MORE PRAISE FOR *HER INFINITE VARIETY*

"A delightful collection . . . shimmers with intelligence and understanding. Berkman's prose quietly and powerfully evokes what so often remains unspoken."
—C. J. Hribal, author of *The Clouds in Memphis*

"An exciting, audacious book. Berkman's daring, novelistic storytelling lifts these women out of their roles in history and gives them their full humanity."
—Kevin McIlvoy, author of *Hyssop*

"A book of great charm, fun to read, and brightly imagined."
—Joan Silber, author of *In My Other Life: Stories*

HER INFINITE VARIETY

STORIES OF SHAKESPEARE AND
THE WOMEN HE LOVED

Pamela Rafael Berkman

SCRIBNER PAPERBACK FICTION
PUBLISHED BY SIMON & SCHUSTER
NEW YORK LONDON TORONTO SYDNEY SINGAPORE

SCRIBNER PAPERBACK FICTION
Simon & Schuster, Inc.
Rockefeller Center
1230 Avenue of the Americas
New York, NY 10020

SCRIBNER PAPERBACK FICTION and design are trademarks of
Macmillan Library Reference USA, Inc., used under license by
Simon & Schuster, the publisher of this work.

Designed by Colin Joh
Text set in Aldus

Manufactured in the United States of America

1 3 5 7 9 10 8 6 4 2

Library of Congress Cataloging-in-Publication Data is available.

ISBN 0-7432-1255-X

To Mehran, my Persian prince

Contents

Gold

Mary Shakespeare, born Mary Arden, wife of John Shakespeare, knelt in the Sunday light before the dark boxwood crucifix in her bedchamber, the same chamber in which she had shielded her oldest surviving child, William, from the plague that raged within two doors of their house when he was only six months old. Her back to the door, as it was now, the rushes on the floor making their imprints on her knees, she had wept and wept those days, in a fury at her helplessness and paralysis to do anything real, anything of scientific merit to keep her baby safe. Two doors away the horrid pestilence was, she knew; the miasma insinuated itself into the blood of her neighbors, into her dear friends' children, rendering them up dead and swollen with the blue-black lumps, like things less than human.

The Virgin had delivered her and her son. Her prayers were answered, and the infection passed over their door, left their home untouched. She had dared not leave their house those days. And now, when she did dare, she could not venture to church. None of the family could, by command of her husband. She could not speak to the Virgin as she so loved to do. In her mind's eye she knelt before the image at Saint Peter's Bishopton, just north of town. She could not there this Sunday silently tell Our Lady all the daily small affairs and accounts of her wifely life, hear her comfort, honor her as she had promised she would do every Sunday her whole life long if only the Mother of God would take pity on her, as a woman, and spare her baby. Through more than ten years, even when ill or indisposed herself, Mary Shakespeare had kept this promise. And now, through no doing of hers, it was broken.

Mary thought of the floor of the church, harder than this one in her bedroom, made of stone with no rushes to ease the knees. It was that floor where she should be, she thought, hard or no. Would it be just the same to the Virgin, to talk to her here in her bedroom? Mary did not know.

She kept her hands folded and her head bowed, next to the simple bed filled with straw that took up most of the small room. The sun streamed in over her through the window—just a shuttered square cut in the wall, no glass to bend the light. She shifted her weight to the balls of her feet under her plain dress, dyed hunter green with the grasses of the river. She was a good wife; she had tried to help her husband as a woman should, and she thought of the Holy Mother in Judea, who despite her exalted state in the eyes of the Father must have helped to see to Joseph's carpentry accounts. Mary Shakespeare herself worked her embroidery, so fine, all over the gloves John Shakespeare made, stitched feathers and knots and creeping vines of blue and yellow, no gold or silver or purple, of course—those colors were by law not for common folk such as them and their fellow villagers, not for folk who might find themselves having to hide from their neighbors on a Sunday instead of going to church with the decent people to adore the Virgin and Saint Francis and Saint Peter, who held the keys to heaven. No. Those silks were only for the queen and those near her, those who might never want for money. Yet blue and yellow, red and green, black silk and pure white, and the mustard color stewed out of the garden onions—remarkable riches could be made of all these things.

Mary did her duty. It was the wool that undid her husband, the wretched wool. She told him not to dabble in the wool dealing, not to hoard it and risk the wrath of the county magistrate and the fine, the sum of which left her breathless. But he said, "Why need you always be so very safe, dear, playing by all the set-down laws and rules? A man does get ahead by breaking such rules, you should know that, wife." Indeed, her own father had broken such rules, in similar escapades and with mixed results. Mary had not liked that, either. To whom did she and her sisters go crying when they were hungry, suffering from his temporary setbacks and his need to appear more wealthy than he was? Not their father. No. It was Mama, dear ma'am; that was who they asked for their dinner. As would her own five children.

"I am afraid, Queen of Heaven," she whispered to the Virgin, though it was the Virgin's son before her eyes on the crucifix on the whitewashed wall. "I am afraid. For what if we are found out, in our absence from church? And we surely will be, and then there will be another fine, and who shall pay *that*?"

"Who shall pay what, ma'am?" asked her boy William,

eleven years old and just beginning to look sturdy, but still with the skinny legs of a young chicken. He had quietly come into the room as she stayed kneeling before God.

He saw how the gold of the sun pouring in through the window fell upon the dark simple green of her gown, her Sunday gown, which she would wear to honor the Lord whether she went to church or no. And he saw that the gold was like embroidery.

"You should wear a pelisse stitched so, Mama, with the sun," he said, and was so happy to see her smile. A great stone dissolved within his heart to see it.

"Such fancies you always have, son," she said.

"My father bids me tell you something," he said, kneeling beside her. He found himself unsure of whether to clasp his hands to pray or no. He was not sure he had anything to say to the Lord.

"Aye?"

"He says, by way of comfort, 'tis only the service of the heretical church, not the one holy faith of your mother and father, and of his mother and father, and so do not mind it too much that we cannot go."

"He does not know my heart, does he? He does not understand, does he, Will?"

William did not answer for a moment. His father fed him and clothed him and gave him his blessing in the morning, and as John Shakespeare would have things be, so his son William dutifully obeyed, as the Bible instructed him. Disobedience was a grave sin. It had led to the fall of man.

But he whispered, "No, ma'am." He had never done such a disrespect to his father before.

"Today is the day to pray to the Virgin and her holy son and pledge again our devotion, whether their image be before us or no," his mother said, her eyes fixed down. Mary so wanted, today, to see the statue of Saint Francis. He was the favorite saint of her grandmother, her grandmother on the Webbe side, who paid the fine, or sometimes defiantly did not pay it, so as not to attend the heretical service. Grandmother Webbe was ever loyal to the old faith. And there were yet statues not destroyed at little Saint Peter's—beside the creamy painted wood of Francis, so simple in his earthy-shaded robes, there was the image of the Mother and Child, in ivory and soft blue. They were kind, these images. Mary Shakespeare was certain of it.

"Yes, ma'am," said her son. But he could see the unhappiness in the lines of her mouth and face, so listless, looking neither angry nor sad but only empty. He could bear it no longer and cried out, "But do not make yourself uneasy, ma'am! My father fears not meeting the Lord, only his creditors. Surely the Lord knows this and can see into your heart. Surely He does not condemn us for our obedience. I am sure that it is godly; obedience is the greatest of virtues, so I have learned in school. That is right, is it not, Mother?"

"I shall tell you a secret, Will." She relaxed her humble kneeling, sitting back, unfolding her hands, and gathered him near her. She wondered, as she always did, from where he had come by the soft warm brown of his hair—her own was a jet black, thick and wavy, and his father even now had almost no hair at all. She said, "I do not know what is right. I am afraid."

William sat very still. He felt his mother's breath against

his cheek. It always carried such a sweet scent, always made him feel he had come home, even if he had not gone away at all and was home already. Her breath smelled a little of milk and a little of perfume, which mystified his mind, curious even now, for he knew she had no such luxury as perfume.

Now he knew what to say to the Lord. He pulled away from his mother, folded his hands, and bowed his head, and spoke silently and fervently to God. He saw that this pleased her.

"Ma'am, I shall not be a glover," he suddenly said, and his voice sounded sharp to him, cutting through the silence of the prayers in the room.

"What are you talking of, William?" And she turned from the image on the wall. "Your father is a glover. He would have you be a glover. What do you mean, you shall not be a glover?"

His voice shook with his fear of his own boldness. What if his father should hear him? "I shall not be a glover." He could not get what he wanted from the Lord if he were a glover.

Mary stroked his soft hair and spoke gently. "We will talk of it another time." And she began again to pray. So did her son.

Pray you, heavenly Father, he thought. Riches. Send me gold.

Gold to pay his father's debts, gold thread for his mother—and a claim to be worthy to wear it. A coat of arms! Yes, gold to buy a coat of arms for his family, why not? Stranger things were done in the city. Gold to make his mother unafraid. Rubies and emeralds and silver and purple cloth and perfume—oh, but mostly gold. O Lord let me earn gold. Gold.

His mother prayed all day in the light of the sun. So did William.

"Father, may I speak?" said William at supper that night, over the ale they all drank. His mother looked up, as did his sisters, Joan and Anne, and his brother Gilbert. Baby Richard was not yet old enough to stand up with the other children at table.

"Yes, son?"

"I shall not be a glover. Or a wool dealer," said William.

His father tensed. "What do you mean, boy?"

"I shall go to the city and do something else."

"What is the meaning of this?"

Will bent his head in deference, but went on. "Father, I shall help the family. I shall be able to discharge our debts and get fine clothes for Mother, and then we may go to church—"

"You shall not!" his father thundered, his voice crashing over William. "Mend your speech! So young, and so untender? Wife, do you complain even to our children of my misfortune in the wool?"

"You know I do not, husband," she said mildly.

"You shall go from this table!" he shouted at Will. "To your bed!"

"Yes, Father." The boy turned to obey, to go upstairs to the little room at the top of the house where all the children slept on one large straw-filled pallet.

"All of you!" his father cried.

They obediently followed, Joan gathering up the baby, all sending dagger looks at their older brother.

"Look not at me that way, wife," said John Shakespeare. "What is it you wish to say?"

"You know my thought on this already, John."

"Tell it."

"You are too severe. He is old enough to be worrying, he wishes to be of use. He is a good boy."

"As he should be, with all his advantages. He might have been a farmer's son, scratching in dirt, as I was! Has he ever had to boil and scrape the refuse of animals from their skins, to sell, as I did for my father? He has not. I rallied myself, I made myself a tradesman. He will be a merchant, he will not be at the mercy of the sun and rain, as were my father and I! A free grammar school in the town! I never had such. And it is my old position on the council that sends him there! You remember"—here he softened—"you remember, my dear, how I used to not like to see you read the accounts, because I could not?"

"But no more. You have got used to it. And you need for me to do so."

"Aye." He considered. "I need for you to do so." He looked at her as she began to clear the table, stack the wooden plates and tankards to be taken out to the kitchen yard for washing, save the bread and cheese the children had had to leave uneaten, and he could not take his eyes from her. Her waist, when she turned and bent and gathered, was as it had been the first day he saw her, with her father in Stratford, bartering chicks for butter with his own father, her father's tenant. Her hair was still just as black. She had come to his house at seventeen, from her father's place in Wilmcote. John had freed her, at least, from the life of a farm, such a hard place for a woman. He had given her a world of merchants and town instead. He was glad he had been able to give her that, glad to be able to give something. And in return, for eighteen years now, she had run his house, helping with his business, embroidering his gloves with those fine-lady stitches of hers. She kept the kitchen, the poultry, the children, everything in irreproachable order. Once he had asked how she could do so many things at once, and she smiled up at him—he was a large and substantial man—and said it must be through the intercession of the Holy Mother.

She knew how he looked at her. She knew, when she saw him first, that he had never before seen a girl like her. Her father, being in one of his more fortunate periods, was then a wealthy farmer, not a scratcher like John's father, and he kept up an illusion of even more wealth than he had. His daughter's skin was delicate, her speech quiet and restrained. She wore a piece of jewelry on market day, a very small silver cross on a ribbon about her neck.

John caught her waist as she turned to the table and buried his face against her. Relief flooded through him as she bent to stroke his hair. "I am sorry about the wool," he said. "You were right, Mary. It was too uncertain an enterprise. I am sorry."

"Well," she answered. And she bent down to look into his face. "If Our Lord and his Mother can forgive, then so can I." She was not yet smiling, but he had hopes.

"I *will* make amends. I *will* deliver us from this debt."

She nodded. "But we cannot continue not to mark the Lord's Day. You must at least allow me to take the children. I cannot continue. I am—in fear." Her mouth became a line and she looked away, over his shoulder. This was real to her, and he needed to know it. "I would not disobey but I must go to church."

He only nodded.

She stood up briskly.

"Say something to your son," she said. "He only wanted to assist you, husband. He is a child, he has fancies."

John Shakespeare sighed and rose, tired, to his feet. "As you wish, my dear."

He strode—his step was never light nor small, he could not help that—into the children's room. The littler ones—Anne, Gilbert, Richard—were asleep, but he thought Joan only feigned slumber, and Will did not pretend at all. The boy was dry eyed and dignified.

"Son," said John, softening his loud, confident voice with effort, "come and stand up now."

William obeyed.

"You are a good boy. You wish to help. But such things are best left to your father. Do you hear me?"

"Yes, sir." But he fidgeted, and he could not help bursting out, "But I will buy us a coat of arms in the city, Father. For you. And for Mother."

"Well, we shall see, son. Go to sleep now."

"Yes, sir."

Mary Shakespeare heard it all, the voices drifting down the stairs. As her husband came back into the dining parlor, smiling, pleased to have pleased her, she thought she saw her life

stretching out both behind and before her, all that had brought
her to this point and all that would come, a path that shone like
a river, but not silver, no, it was the color of the sun. She saw
the point, eleven years ago, when she gave birth—gave it, a
gift—to her son and became, at least in some way, like her
namesake, the Holy Virgin. And she thought she saw a place,
far in the future, when he would part from her and take
some shining path himself, and she saw also the point where
he would part from this world and go into the next, and perhaps, she thought, she hoped, she believed, in this and in all
things, the Virgin would guide him.

And her son, in his bed, prayed again, for her, for gold.

In the Bed

Anne Shakespeare, a swirl of rolling circles, bounced up and down atop her husband, driving him deeper and deeper inside her, the night before he left for London. Her body was still all made of circles, just as it had been the day he noticed it and his life changed, became a circle around the center of her, when he was twelve and the realization of her roundness burst upon him outside Saint Peter's Bishopton, the Stratford church. She was already twenty then.

That day he watched her beneath the sun, saw her moving this way and that, attending to her little brothers and sisters, but in his mind there was only the flash of dozens of circles, as he had seen her when she walked past his family that morning in her plain blue gown and sat two rows before them, on the left side of the aisle. She smelled like April and May.

Her eyes were blue, blue shining disks in the circle of her face. Her breasts were soft spheres. There were no almond shapes, no teardrops; everything about her was like the moon and the sun. Her belly, round and beautiful. Yes, like a heap of ripe wheat. And around the edges of the wheat . . . he imagined how her belly sloped downward toward the joints of her thighs, how there, there must be shining red-gold down, softer than the brilliant red-copper floss she piled in intricate looping braids on top of her head. Below her waist spread the perfect curve of her hips, which seemed the true center of her body, from which everything else emanated in warm, inviting motions. The shapes were light and overlapped, and shone like a cluster of wet, translucent grapes, moving easily around and above and below one another. Her elbows were smooth spots of cream. Her mouth seemed round as a rose and pink, and the plums of her cheeks were pink as well. Even the tip of her nose ended in its own tiny upturned circle.

On this night she laughed atop him in the bed, and he laughed too. At first he found her laughter at such moments disconcerting, those years ago before they married, before the children were born—he was feeling terribly serious, what on earth was funny?—but not anymore.

"What ... amuses ... you ... my ... love?" he asked, one word with every lively thrust, until her giggles dissolved into soundless sighs and her face flushed with satisfaction, so that he too stopped holding back and gave in to his own arousal.

"You have killed me, Nan," he said as she rolled off him and he lay immobile and watery. "Now I cannot leave tomorrow. You have had your way after all."

She propped herself up on one elbow next to him. This bed, in his father's house, was simple and small, with sheets of undyed plain stuff that rustled crisply beneath them when their bodies moved. She did not laugh or smile.

"You know that is not true," she said. "You know I wish you were not to go, but if you feel it is for our betterment, you must. You know that is not true."

"Aye, sweetheart, forgive me, I tease you. You know I tease you."

"It is an odd thing to do, you must own. People do not leave their homes, Will. My brother Bartholomew would not stay in the village, it is true. He married and went to Isabel's home at Tysoe, but most people do not do that, you must own."

"I can write to the family. My mother could read you the letters." His father could not read, but his mother could, a little. "Or Susanna may be able to, in time." He was playing with her hair. It was so red. He tried very hard not to remind her that he could read and she could not, but tonight he wanted to tell her he would write.

"Will you stay away so long? She will not read for some years."

The sheets rustled, stiff and scratchy. "Ah. No. Well, I do not plan, my love, we spoke of that, you know, I do not know. It depends upon the success I find. I should like to do well in the company, Nan. I should like to be able to send you some substantive portion of money. Perhaps I may be able, in time, to earn enough that we need no longer live in my father's house. I should like for you to be mistress of your own home. I should like for you to have everything you want."

Then he sat up. "I shall not go," he suddenly said. "I would rather speak to you than write to you. I shall not go."

"No, Will. You shall. I will not have you here, always wondering. I'll have you leave tomorrow."

She stretched and reached out her hand to play with the gold ring in her husband's ear. It had been her earring long ago, before she had lost the mate and given it to him, piercing his ear in the parlor of her own father's house when he was fifteen. He had sat on the wooden stool, gripping the edge of the seat, his feet tense on the rush-covered floor. The sun streamed in. Her entire family was there, her sisters giggling, her stepmother hushing them, holding in her arms the youngest infant son. And Burman, who was so much older and wealthy, was there too, and Reynolds. They had all converged upon her parlor that May afternoon. For surely, in Stratford or Shottery, there was never a woman more beautiful than Anne Hathaway.

But only young Will Shakespeare would consent to let her pierce his ear.

She held the sewing needle and the cork.

"I have heard that all the gentlemen of London wear a gold ring in the ear," she said.

"I am not in London," he answered.

"Please, Master Shakespeare! It will make you look older."

How could he refuse her anything? He screwed up his eyes and gripped the stool harder while Burman guffawed. "Punch!" he cried.

The needle went through. At first it felt only like someone was pinching his earlobe, but then the pinch was harder, and harder, and harder, and did not let up, and his eyes teared, and finally there was a sickening, low pop, and his ear was pierced. It flashed hot when she put in the ring.

"Do not take it out, now," she had said.

Now, his head on her pillow, Will said, "It was good you did that, was it not? I shall look a city gentleman, in London."

"Yes." She laughed. "You went quite white."

"I was quite ill."

He was thinking of the parlor, and of May.

"You were the best of the dancers on May Day, always," he said.

"Aye," she said, smiling slowly. "I was." When she danced her hips swayed and bounced, swiveled and bopped, her breasts laced up tight like plump fruit in a basket. He could not help but look at what was in the basket. The ribbons shone on her holiday dress. Such confidence she had, stepping perfectly right on the beat of the drummers, knowingly slapping her hip at just the right moment in the pause.

"I remember wanting to give you a present," he said. "I remember wondering what you would like. I thought perhaps I would bring you ribbons."

"But you brought me gloves."

"I remember. My father made them. I saw you walking into the forest with Burman."

"You knew I had lovers at May Days."

"But I called to you, just the same."

"You spoke well then. Your beard was still so soft."

"I had one at last." And he certainly was speaking well then. All that rhetoric, absorbed as he sat on that hard wooden plank at grammar school, had taken seed within him and blossomed. His beard grew soft and brown, and he was not so skinny anymore. He called to her, at the revels the May he was eighteen, though she was by Burman's side, "Lady, do you hate me?" To which she replied, surprised, "Indeed, sir, I hate you not." And he said, "Lady, from heaven to hell is flown away: I hate, from hate away she threw, and saved my life saying, 'Not you.' "

It was from a sonnet he wrote her and kept among his notebooks in his father's shop, hidden away where none could find it, in accounts only he could or would try to make head or tail of. He was trying to make a pun out of her last name: hate away, Hathaway. It was not very good as a pun, he admitted to himself at the time, but perhaps he would get better. And she looked at him as though he were new to her, someone in the village who had not been there before.

Now he said softly, his face in her hair, "It made great sense to me when you said you were with child, that Susanna was coming." All that roundness. Of course she would bring forth a warm, plump child.

After that he had to ride in the cold of November to the bishop's court at Worcester with two of her father's cronies, Fulke Sandelles and John Richardson, who were none too pleased with him, the boy who had dishonored their late upstanding friend's daughter. But he returned with the license, and they were married the last Sunday before December, the only chance they would have for weeks, as there could be no weddings during Advent. His mother was pleased that he had acquitted himself well and done the proper thing—she liked Anne—and he, of course, was pleased that his mother was pleased. Anne's party were more somber about the event.

"Sandelles and Richardson would not speak to me the entire journey, you know that, lady."

She sat up so she could let the fringe of her hair fall over his chest, a river of red and gold in the sputtering candle-light. They had left the candle to burn all night. They liked to see each other.

"You have told me, my love. How very uncomfortable for you. Perhaps you should have demonstrated some restraint with me, those summer nights at the bend of the river."

"How could I?"

"Better our daughter, my dear, than what might have been."

"What?"

"Davy says the man who left Lord Strange's troupe to make room for you has the clap. He says players in London are terrified of the clap."

Davy Jones was her kinsman, who put on mummers' shows. He was marginally acquainted with two of the younger members of the Earl's Men, the troupe sponsored by Lord Strange. They stopped at Stratford that year. Will was to leave with them.

"Nan, I shall not—" he began.

She said, "I opened the door for you. I taught you to love a woman."

"It is not my aim—"

"We sometimes fall into that which is not our aim."

"Listen. Listen. I am very skilled at poetry. More skilled than I am at anything else. I am a good player. I have a mind to try my hand at being a theater poet. I think I can bring us some consequence in the world, some prosperity. Perhaps enough to leave my father's house. If not, I will return, I swear."

"The twins are only two. Will they remember you, when

you return?" She sounded as though she were only idly wondering. Something in his heart again said, I shall not go, but he did not voice it. She had said she would have him leave tomorrow.

"I shall at least come for a month," was all he answered, "before the year is out."

"Yes. Do come before the year is out. Come soon."

He wanted to change the subject.

"I believe I can be effective, writing for the theater," he said. "I have been thinking over something. I have some idea of how to improve my work."

"Yes? Tell me, let us talk of it, so I shall know what you are thinking of in the city."

"Well," he began. He was not sure she would understand, as she could not read a poem, although she had twice seen a play, when the Earl's Men came to Stratford.

"Mmm?" she murmured.

"To keep the interest of the people coming to see the players," he said, "when the poet tells the story, it is not enough to simply tell the story. There are two points to a story, you see, good and bad, or life and death, or some such opposing problem. And the people in the story move through it, and come to an end of it. But that is not enough, it is not enough to tell only about those two things. Those who have come to see the play will not be satisfied. They will know things ahead of time, they will not have the delight of surprise, here and there. The story will be too easy, they will not perceive any danger, or consequence. There must be a third point, something from outside, to put more strain upon the story that is being told. Do you understand?"

"Oh, yes, my dear. It is like the story of Tristram and Isolt that the German troubadour told when last the mummers came. It is not enough that Isolt drinks the magic potion and loves Tristram, and he her, and then they must be apart and then together. She must also be betrothed and then married to Tristram's dearest friend, King Mark. That is the third point. Yes?"

He was so pleased. "Yes. And I have just realized this to be true. And now I shall never write anything without it, this other point, and every verse I write shall be better."

"Yes, my love." She kissed his forehead. The room was getting cold. The sky was a charcoal gray now, the chilly light showing through the slits in the shutters, and a harsh bird's song sounded. Anne rose to put on her nightdress. She suddenly bent to kiss him on the mouth, surprising him. She kissed him as though it were for the last time, as though she were bidding him farewell forever.

"No, no, that was a nightingale you heard," he said. "It is not morning yet."

"You know right well it is, Will Shakespeare. It was a lark."

He always swept her into his arms and his great heavy cloak when he returned, so all her circles were wrapped up in his. There were beautiful women in London, and he was finding how much he liked women, but it was her he wanted. Truly. Only, he had not known there was so much room in a man's heart, so many places. He did meet women who were not like Anne, not like any woman he had ever seen in Stratford or Shottery. He had a friend whose wife wrote poetry herself, as finely wrought as that of an educated man. And another, little Nell, had quite a sack of tricks to her credit but somehow never seemed other than innocent. He told himself that he used his English common sense in matters of London ladies; he was not debauched, like some of the other players. He was only a man away from home, a man who wanted for his wife and whom ladies found pleasant. "I miss you, I miss you," he called as he swirled Anne about.

He sent her pretty things from London. Beads, a mirror. He was careful to return for at least one month's time every year. He made money. He bought her a house.

"New Place," he said to her. "Do you remember how we all used to admire it, on the way to school?" But of course, he momentarily forgot that she had not gone to school. Still, it was the most beautiful, biggest house in the neighborhood, and he gave it to her, and she smiled on him. He bought new furniture for it, too, an elaborate carved bed with rich hangings—she had it put into a bedroom for guests—joined stools and a table for the hall, and carpets. "I want you to have whatever you wish for," he said. "Everything you want."

"And how is school?" he said on his first night home to his son, Hamnet, the year the boy was ten. The newly returned master sat before the fire drinking hot punch his mother had made while his family clustered, standing, about him.

"Fine, so please you, sir," said Hamnet, shy with his father, hanging his head like one much younger.

"Oh now, my boy," said old John Shakespeare to his grandson. "'Fine, so please you, sir,' does he answer! Surely it is not so fine as that? Do you remember, Will, how you griped and miseried about your master to me? Not that you ever had any sympathy from me; no, not then and not now. 'Twas a fine advantage to you, and look what a success you have made of your learning! But sure I never heard you call it 'fine' to me."

"Poor boy, in the throes of grammar school," said Will, smiling, and left it at that. "Do you ask for your grandsire's blessings in the mornings, Hamnet, when I am not here?" And the boy buried his head against his grandfather's leg.

John patted his shoulder. "Aye, son, he does. He is a good boy, a good boy. Very obedient to his mother."

Will heard a motion that night, in his sleep, and woke to find himself alone.

"Nell?" he called softly, before he remembered he was home again. Then, horrified, he sat up, jolted at the thought that his wife must have heard him. But she was not in the room. Where was his warm Anne? He went to the door and looked into the hall. She was not there, either.

In the kitchen he saw her. She had lit a rush light. He had brought home a draft of something he was working on, a story of two lovers, Romeo and Juliet, with many blottings out and crossed-out lines. She was looking at it by the candlelight, turning page after page, gazing at the magic markings she could not understand. He backed away from the kitchen door, went back upstairs to their bed.

The next morning she was careful to wear the lace he had brought her. He watched her stitching the children's clothes in the sunlight in the large airy parlor. He would be rich, truly rich, in the near future; that was certain now. She need

sew then only if she wanted to. Then, he could give her anything she wanted.

They both looked at their son from the window.

"He is not easy with me," said Will.

"That is his age," Anne answered. "He talks of you all the
time when you are away from home."

Did he hear, for the first time, a sharpness in the words
"away from home"? No. Not from Anne. Surely that was
only his fancy. Still, he felt a need to say something for himself.

"I know you are all left much in the care of my father and
your brother," he said. "I only wish . . . I wish to provide
things for you, Anne, for you all. Like this house. Surely this
house gives you pleasure? I do not want you and my mother
to think of me as a poor, disreputable player."

"We never thought of you so."

This was true. He knew it as soon as she said it.

"But the town may, and I would have neither of you bear
such a burden. I want no one to say you are the wife of
William Shakespeare, the player. I want all to say you are
the wife of William Shakespeare, the poet and gentleman, of
New Place."

She did not answer him. She looked away from him and
back to Hamnet, who had found his friend Thomas Quiney's
puppy and was teasing it, holding one end of a large stick in
his hand while the pup worried the other end between its
teeth, growling occasionally and unthreateningly.

"I like to have him about me," she said to Will. "He is like
you were."

Will smiled. He was. Skinny, with a high forehead, gray

eyes, and soft brown hair. The girls had neither of them got their mother's beauty, though Susanna was fair and would be pleasant looking. Hamnet's twin, Judith, was a puzzle. She would be tall, but she was very thin and dark, and quiet.

Will Shakespeare looked at his wife. She was still so lovely. Her hair still thick and shining copper, her breasts and hips still so smooth and full, all the shapes still moving so elegantly together.

Will and Anne could not sleep in their own bed the next time he came home from London. That very afternoon Hamnet wandered in from the kitchen yard, where he had been playing at running games with his sisters and cousins.

"Mother," he said, finding her overseeing a kettle slung over the kitchen fire. "May I sit, ma'am? I do not want to stay in the yard."

"Are you feeling poorly?"

"No, ma'am, I cannot tell why, I only do not wish to be outside, I should like to sit."

His father, hearing them from the hall, where he had been refreshing himself with ale after his journey, entered. "Son? Just home from school and you wish to sit?"

"Aye, so please you, sir."

"Well, you may sit," said his mother. She boiled him an egg and put it before him on the wood plank table.

"Mother, may I eat it later?"

She looked at him, felt his wrists and face. "He is damp, husband, and look."

Will looked into his son's eyes and saw them glittering, unfocused.

"Bed," he said.

Anne put Hamnet in their own bedchamber, the warmest in the house, and Will and young Samuel, the servant, moved the bed closer to the fire. Ever careful, she sent the girls to her brother's home—Bartholomew had come back to Stratford—and as the boy began to babble that evening and finally ceased to speak at all, only whimpered sometimes, she told the housekeeper, Mary Quickly, who no doubt already knew, that later the bedding would have to be burned. Together the women brewed the herbs their mothers had used for such afflictions: garlic and goldenseal for the fever, mustard and mint for the lungs.

"I do not wish to call for old Rogers," Anne said to her husband in the kitchen, her face damp from the steam of the pots. She meant Philip Rogers, the apothecary. "He is honest enough, but . . ."

"No, no, I understand you perfectly, my dear, we will send for a physician at once." And as if to demonstrate his resolve to do so, Will emptied his purse into his hand and showed her the money in it, enough to pay for any doctor or surgeon. "There, you see, our son shall have the best care."

"Yes. I am glad. Send Samuel for him, now."

On the fifth day the physician had not yet arrived for that morning's visit to his little patient. Anne still held the money in coins her husband had given her to pay him when he came.

Unspecified fever—who knew exactly what it was? An elixir had been recommended, which Master Shakespeare lost no time in purchasing, thanking God at the time that he was in a position to do so, thinking it would save his son, and yet knowing in the back of his mind that many, many children could not be saved. The physician had been every morning and every night for three days, and last night it had not looked well, but he had been summoned to another child with similar symptoms. And then this morning, when Hamnet's breath sounded like a rattle in his skinny chest, the physician was sent for again. No doubt he came in haste and was on his way.

But the boy was dead.

Will and Anne stayed with him, as though by pre-arranged agreement, though there was none. They were both reluctant to leave him alone, as though he could still feel lonely and ask for his mother and father. They had been married fourteen years. Their lives were already hopelessly intertwined, impossible to tease apart.

She looked up at him, her eyes not round, but narrow lines, a shape in which he had never known them. This time, for the first time, she looked at him with hate.

It is not her fault, he kept saying to himself. She is destroyed, she knows not what she does or says. But the look changed something in him that never changed back, though he kept waiting for it to, though she never again looked at him so viciously. She was teaching him, as she always had, but this time it was lessons he did not want, about loss and death and precious things broken that could not fit seamlessly back together.

"I want my son, that is what I want," she hissed at him. Then, more loudly, "I want my son!" She threw the coins for the doctor and his potions at her husband and walked from the room as they rolled about the floor. And her back as she walked was rigid, and her body full of corners. She shut the door hard behind her.

Magic Wand

I am a tiny little thing, of course, being that most royal and dazzling Titania, queen of the fairies, and I spend most of my time in the fairy wood among my kind, the Bacchae and the Maenads, and the hobgoblins, and my fairy attendants, Moth and Mustardseed, Cobweb and Peaseblossom, who treat me with the respect I deserve. *Rule, Titania! Titania, rule the waves!* That's me. Nevertheless I sometimes do spy into this rude, mechanical world of mortals, with my fairy second sight, and see something that I must *attend* to, if you see what I mean. And quite an entity I am, when I attend to something, don't underestimate me. So I find myself on oh! this very, very *cold* morning buzzing like a jeweled dragon-fly—I am quite lovely, you know—unseen, unrecognized, and yet not quite unfelt at the ear of young Master Shakespeare in this drafty loft above a dairy while his pen scratch, scratch, scratches away and he hopes for inspiration—that is, though he knows it not, he hopes for *me*.

Poor boy. See how he breathes on his hands every few moments to warm them. I must do something about that, ease his circumstances, but not yet, not just yet.

Pity he can't see me. He likes the ladies, I warrant. And he writes to please a queen, his own queen. I don't think much

38

of her. Cold creature. I'd be a much better queen for him—
there is none of this frozen virgin nonsense about me. I
know how to warm up to my attendants. I'm terribly full of
life, you know, lots of fun. Nothing but fun, fun, fun all day
in the fairy wood, sometimes flitting in and out of the public
houses just for variety. And I do *so* love a poet!

I'm whispering to him, skipping over his inner ear and
going straight into his brain, telling him what to put down
about me. But the dear little freezing lamb, he does not know
the origin of his notions, he just wonders what that odd
sound is, buzzy buzzy buzz, and why won't it leave him in
peace so he can write? *Ow!* Though he cannot feel me, he
swipes at me like I'm a bug every few minutes just the same.
My long-nosed poet with his cold fingers and his scratchy
pen, in this frosty room with the moo-oo-oo-oo of the cows
below, all he can afford. Nothing more than a bunk above a
glorified stable. But that does not concern me now.

Make me immortal again, I murmur to him every few
lines. Without you, dear master poet, sweet master poet,
handsome master poet—well, I shall not even speak it. I can
see all things, and I know.

He didn't know what was wrong with his play at first.
Had my husband, Oberon (hah!), directing everything. I
had barely a line. He had no idea what he needed.

"Estrogen!" I called to him when I saw him at his tiny
writing desk from across the gulf between him and my fairy
reality. And a wave of my golden wand whistled through the
air, swoosh, swoosh, and here I am in his stable of a room.
Hanging from his earlobes, swinging from his earring, carrying moonbeams home in a jar. And aren't I so beautiful,

my wings all of emerald and jade, my body of gold and pearl, pearls of wisdom?

I'm why the ladies will love you so, young sir. Me, that's why. I wooed you. I don't care what anyone says about your dark ladies. Hmph. Not those courtly dowager patronesses in ashes, they never did you the good you deserved. I took you under my pretty wings. Me, that's who—it's all me, me, me! Remember that, when memories of me have gone—but they will not go, if you can continue to hear even a little of me, and if you do your work well, sir.

I've been to see them all. Kyd, Marlowe, Greene. Not a one of them even feels me in the room. And Marlowe has no sense of humor. You won't catch him writing a silly play within a play or poking fun at his own profession. No, he just pulls the bell cord for his landlady and demands she fetch him up some hot cinnamon rolls. Spoiled boy. He can't hear me at all. The university men are all pointless. You'd think with all his darkness Marlowe would be the one to hear me, to understand the hidden depths of the forest, the way the green floor of it once came alive after sundown with night rats and watery snails foraging their food . . . but no. It is clean-living you from the Midlands who pick up my voice from amid all the other clang and clatter.

And don't tell me about Spenser and his pale transparent imitation of me. S-o-o-o filmy . . . None of my deep, jewel-like colors, all sapphire and starlight I am—did I say before I was emerald and jade? Well, I change. Like a chameleon. That's me, I'm a changeable woman. "Ivory white," he called me—I am not ivory white! My toes, you know, are as rosy as little carbuncles.

So, swoosh, swoosh, on the wings of the air I came straightaway to you, young Shakespeare. To whisper pearls into your ear, pearls to cast before swine and groundlings, pearls to strew onto your paper. Poor unrecognized young man, in your spindly-furnished little room in Cheapside, with the chickens and cows just downstairs and nothing but straw to sleep in. But your skin is very smooth . . .

Oh now, how sweet, aren't you just giving me the prettiest speeches? Listen to me telling the moon, the governess of floods, to wash all the air! I'm *so good*! Oh, give me such things to say, you master of words, pretty, pretty things! There is such power in words. That's what I want, sir mortal. Don't pay me my homage in gold, or diamonds, or jewels from the deep. Why do you think I ignore those silly rich noblemen? What can *they* give me that I can't conjure up with my very own wand? Send me my tribute in words!

Ah, how you labor, my poor base creature, how your pen scrapes. I sigh. Were it me, a quick swooshy wave of my wand and the pages would all be finished, stacked neatly there, perhaps dusted lightly with gold bullion, just as a little fairy greeting. It could all be done. But mortals can never see my handiwork in this day and age . . . and it will be worse in the future. I am already changed—I was not always pink and silver and netting, like a little ballerina's play tutu, in men's minds. So undignified and inelegant. I was once made of truer colors, dark wine red, green so deep men saw their faces reflected in it, and orange raw gold with the earth still clinging to it. That was in the old days, when I walked the earth by day as much as by night.

But never you mind, young man. You give voice to me,

and I will ensure that you at least can speak from the grave. Marlowe, Bacon, even your queen—you will rise and rise until you shine above them all like the sun over the postcards at the Stratford Birthplace!

And swoosh with my wand! Consider it done.

Now, then. As to Oberon, the fairy king. A fine figure, indeed, with his Asian eyes and shimmering blue silken robes, but must you make him my husband? *Ow!* Don't swat at me, sir, beside your ear, or swoosh, swoosh, and I'll conjure you up a case of writer's block to last the millennium. . . . Oberon, I will have you know, is my brother. I will never marry! It was not necessary for beings like us. . . . I remember, in the thick of the ancient greenery, full of eyes, eyes to watch my Oberon when he pursued me and took me, that May before there was history or time or even May. My brother and I, slick as eels, moving together while our own Robin Goodfellow looked on, playing his pipes to celebrate for the gods of the earth . . .

Well, perhaps that is a bit racy for the Elizabethans. Not that they are not racy, as you know, sir, off writing your poems about Venus forcing herself on pretty boys. Still, you may marry me off to Oberon in the play, if you must, young man. I understand the audience might be uncomfortable, though 'twas all commonplace once. You may take poetic license. Ah, mortals are such fools. But really, sir, the human women of your play! They really wish to chain themselves to those swaggering boys? Well. So be it. I know you must please the public. Silly public.

Do you remember, young Shakespeare, your own midsummer nights? Do you remember the nine-men's morris dance? Games and flowers so full of perfume they could enchant the eyes and make a man fall under the spells of love. The handfuls of roses full of the gold dust of the sun, the citrine and carnelian among the violets and oxlips, the cup-shaped breasts of the girls under their blouses and gowns, wet with dew. I was there. I saw it all. You and your wife, young Anne—ah, now that is a woman! Wasn't I there, the queen of the fairies, all in my gold and silver gilt, covered with green leaves softer than petals, hovering like a mosquito above the springtime ponds—I am not bad at imagery myself, sir, though I cannot match your wordplay, your love rising and falling and pointing. I did not have a Latin and Greek education, as you did. No Plutarch or Catullus for me, sir, as I was there when they set the work down, and vastly unimpressed was I. An arrogant bunch. Never showed me proper respect.

But you, sir. Shall I tell you? I can see all that will come. In the future you will be so revered that computer programs (never you mind what that is, sir, that is not the point) will be devised to name the roles you likely acted in your plays! Just for sport, I will make the conclusions incorrect. Swoosh, swoosh.

What's this, young man? What's this? An ass! You have me falling in love with a common weaver with the head of an ass!? I don't care what magic potion claims responsibility, you take that out! You take that out right now! Wipe that smirk off your face!

You have no idea what I will have to put up with a few hundred years hence, when I am almost totally forgotten. I shall be a performance artist—ah, you don't even know what that is, do you? I shall sing songs in a very high voice in the subway! And a subway shall not be a pleasant place! But to this I shall be reduced, to be noticed at all. It shall be very depressing, I assure you, and it shall be all that I can take without this *ass* indignity.

But perhaps I should speak to you more sweetly. Dear Master Shakespeare. Dear handsome, virile Master Shakespeare. Must you? Can't you have one of the mortal women fall in love with the ass and take him away to her bower? Or better yet, Oberon—sometimes he likes men. Can I not wheedle? Can you not hear me? I shall sound my fairy trumpet in your ear. As luck would have it, it is right here. Da-da-da-*duh*! Fanfare, fanfare! Ow! *Stop swiping!* My wings, you ungrateful wretch, are tired, fluttering these hours by your ear in this unheated rented room, whispering things past your eardrum and consciousness and straight into your thoughts. I am I am, I am the fairy queen and I am! So much to be done in fairyland, and here I take the time to see you. True, there's an advantage to me, I won't deny it. But think what I am giving you.

Here. This is what I can give you. Would you like this?

Before me I see—four hundred years hence, across the ocean, where the queen's colonies are—a coffeehouse. Oh, never mind, it's like a tavern, they sell something Italian there called coffee. In the coffeehouse is a boy, limbs sinewy with youth. A pretty boy, he would do well for one of your Violas or your Juliets—ah, you have not written those yet. Well, don't expect me to help you with those.

"How are you?" says the boy to the keeper of the coffeehouse. She brings him a drink, hot, sugary, and sweet—his hair is shorn very close, dear me, he is just lovely. His chest is only beginning to broaden, no hair on it yet, and his shoulders are like those of a young deer. They show through that sleeveless garment he wears, knit of something fine . . . I do not know what they will call that. I could look at him all day. . . .

Ah. Yes. He has a book, which is open. Its cover is such as you, sir, have never seen, soft paper, and shiny. It is a printing of a play. The name of the poet is set in large letters across the cover, larger even than the name of the work. Whose is it? Is it Marlowe's? Is it Kyd's? Nashe, or Greene? It is not. It is William Shakespeare. Name of the son of a country glover. This, I will give you.

That boy is a young player. Very young. He works here, in the coffeehouse. That is why the keeper here knows him and brings him his hot, sweet drinks. He smiles and talks nicely. He worships you.

He is playing a young man, not a woman. In a small production, for no money, Master Shakespeare, none at all, only for love of you. And in front of perhaps a hundred, not your gallery of three thousand. For you.

He plays your tortured prince, your sweet Hamlet. His joy was such when he was told he could play it he called his mother. "Mom," he said—that is the word they will use—"I'm Hamlet." And when she hung up the phone—never mind what that is—she cried for her boy's happiness. He himself has wept upon reading your speeches, quiet so no other boy can see. Sometimes he lets girls see because he is beginning to find they rather like it, but that is beside the point, it is no trick, he weeps. He knows. He knows.

I offer him to you.

Swoosh, swoosh. It is done.

And yet you will not take out my love for the donkey. Traitor. Fine. Sit there making your wood of gentle blues and greens, in which no one can ever be truly lost, where the thin trees sway gently in the breeze beneath the dappled light like on some landscaped university campus full of Frisbees. In time none of you will have any idea of what a wood can be, of what we used to get up to in ours, in the old days, in the night, the drums and the skin, the ice and the fire and the life's blood. Go on. Write this new time's delicate, harmless sprites. You have no idea what will come to pass. But without you and your words, young master, no one will ever hear me again.

A pretty state things have come to, when I beg favors of you!

That ass, young sir, that really cannot stand unanswered. For that—hear me now—there will always be argument on whether your work is yours. Some will say it was Marlowe wrote it, after all. Or Bacon, or even your queen. Or that insufferable de Vere. And why? Because you are not highborn enough for them. So there. My fairy queen's curse on you—no small things, my curses, which can put a princess to sleep for a thousand years from nothing more than the prick of a spindle; my curses, which turn kings to toads and back again. A wave of my wand. Swoosh! Now, you see. And the authorship of your words will be debated forevermore.

But you must not think I will forget you. You give back to me my immortality. I will aid you in yours. That is my fairy queen's reward. Once I could conjure up a kingdom for a man who pleased me. Here, this I give you:

You worry about providing for your wife and children respectably? You shall. And evermore. I can see what the centuries will do for commerce. For all the revenue that you can generate, as well as for your art, you shall live forever, Master Shakespeare. Your profession—hard to believe now, I comprehend—but one day it will be the most ennobled calling in the world, with all the riches of royalty.

And here is what I see:

A tourist attraction. Ah, you do not know what that is. Ice cream is involved. You do not know what that is, either. Well, there is hot sun, sweet sticky things fixing to sidewalks. Knitted shirts, like those the boy was wearing, with your likeness on them. On some of them, you are saying witty things, written in cartoon balloons over your head.

There are plane tickets and theme tours. Your birthplace a shrine of pens and stationery. Christmas tree ornaments and video games for the Americans from the colonies. Cinema. Posters. Key chains. Tea sets. Your words recited in parks, on beaches, below burning suns and starlight, and on dark screens, and in the most ornate of opera houses.

I shall make your very name an industry. And I will give you that sweet boy and thousands like him. He will keep you alive forever. That much I owe you. Swoosh, swoosh.

Really! Must you name the ass *Bottom*? I see you smile, young Master Shakespeare. I see you smile. But without you, I shall surely be no more, and I am sore afraid, deathly afraid. Like you rude mechanicals, I do not want to die. Remember me, as you love me, as you love your home and the greenwood. Remember me.

Swoosh.

Jennet

When she was pregnant with the first baby, Jennet Davenant felt the early twinges in her lower belly with wonder. The spring sky was beautiful and gray, hazy with coming warmth, when first she felt it. There was a bit of twisting and cramping in the first months. The child grew. Amazing. She could even laugh at the nausea she bore, although it would have been easier if she had had sisters, instead of the three brothers, to laugh at it with her. Her brothers came to the house, beaming, with presents. Her husband, John, was a wine importer and merchant, and their home was prosperous and comfortable. It was across the river from the theater, and they could sometimes hear the trumpets in fanfare announcing the performance. They rather liked the theater. John Davenant was intelligent, well schooled, well traveled. He was a modern, sophisticated man.

Jennet's three brothers were an embroiderer, a glover, and a perfumer to the queen. They brought their handiwork—a christening gown like a tiny cloud, a vial of the waters of lavender and roses, and the tiniest pair of gloves you ever did see. Jennet sat in the salon, and her husband sat by her, smiling, a more silly smile than he often wore. He was a quiet sort, much as he liked entertainments and poetry.

Her brothers addressed her belly as Young John.

"It will be a son, indeed it will, good brother," they said to her husband. "Few girls in this family! Only our own little Jennet." Her name was really Jane, she was born Jane Shepard, but her family had always called her Jennet.

"One like her will not displease me," John said.

Jennet smiled, acknowledging this, and then said, "I do wish."

"Yes, sweetheart?"

"That your business did not call you away."

"I am sorry." And he was. "I'll return in plenty of time." John was doing well, as anyone could see from the rich carpets in the room, the polished furniture. But not yet so well that he could afford to have other men see to his affairs.

"We'll be here, brother," said Thomas, the embroiderer. He patted his sister's shoulder, and she felt the turning, turning, turning inside her.

As she grew bigger she began to shine and glow. The third to the sixth month she actually felt quite well—she was only nineteen, and she had always been strong and vital, rosy and full of health. She was never lonely. Her brothers came to see her. She did not really have any women friends, but the servants were of good quality and helpful, and her husband employed a midwife to look in on her regularly. From her windows she could see, being ferried upstream with furled sails, ships like those that carried her husband's wine, casks of gallons and gallons from sun-drenched Bordeaux, on their way to dock at Three Cranes Wharf. She swelled and felt full of the sea, big bellied like a wave, or a sail before the wind, with a little blue-green fish swimming inside of her. She was warm and happy. She thought of names. Elizabeth, she thought, for the queen, if it were a girl—besides, she had always loved the name Elizabeth. Francis for a boy. She liked Saint Francis. It would be Francis John, for her husband, too. By the seventh month she felt heavy and immobile, ready for it all to be over, but still not unwell. One day, the ships being ferried upstream to Three Cranes were her husband's ships, and the servant came in carrying a note:

My dear wife,
All went well, I am safely returned, my own boat will be in harbor this evening tide. I will be arriving home some hours after.

She had a supper made, something simple to his liking—he was not a large eater—boiled eggs, some cold meat. Then she waited on the parlor sofa.

She must have dozed. She awoke to hear the housekeeper say, "Thanks be you are safely returned, sir," and her husband's warm voice replying something, and then he was in the room before she could bestir herself to sit up.

She did, however, and smiled. He stopped at the edge of the sofa. There was a soft parcel under his arm, done up in butcher's paper. She looked down at her girth.

"Are you shocked, husband?"

"No," he said. "No." He leaned to kiss her delicately, so

gently, on the cheek. Then he stood back again. "I have brought you something." He handed her the parcel—one of the corners had already peeled back and showed red silk, gold thread.

"Dear husband, I am not sure what I can fit into . . . ," she said. Had he forgotten, in all those months, that when he came home she would not be the delicate little creature he knew? Did she perhaps repel him in her present state? Men, so proud to be fathers, seemed to have such a horror of actual childbirth and all associated with it.

"Unwrap it, you will see," he said.

She did. It was a Chinese robe, red and gold and peacock, shimmering like the noon sun—and it was gigantic.

She stood up and pulled it over her plain gown, laughing, and he laughed too. It was big enough for her now, and with room to spare. She caught her arms round his neck. "My husband," she said. She liked to hear the words.

He was home when the pains struck, and sent a boy for the midwife as the maids helped her into bed. Things seemed to progress quickly, and Jennet took this as a good sign, but she did wish the midwife would hurry. The baby seemed a little early, by her reckoning.

The midwife came. The room was full of the cold daylight that streamed in through thin muslin draperies, yet was somehow oppressive—the wood panels had never seemed so dark, the rich rugs never so suffocating.

"Goodwife Reynolds, I fear something is not right," Jennet called out from her feathery bed. "It moved very quickly and now it has stopped, Goodwife Reynolds, it feels quite heavy." She would not say "leaden." She would not say "dead."

"Yes, my dear," said Goodwife Reynolds, who was used to alarmed young mothers. But her face was unreadable as she felt beneath the sheets, there were no words of reassurance, and her voice became clipped and hard as she told Jennet to push.

"What?" said Jennet.

"Push, my dear. Think: Blessed Virgin, push, Blessed Virgin, push. That's better. Blessed Virgin . . ." Oh, why would the midwife not close her mouth? She knew to push.

It took so long, and Jennet rode wave after wave of pain. She knew the baby was stillborn long before it was out of her and there was no cry. The midwife was rough with it. Jennet could tell her only concern was to extract it from her body. She was delirious with the twisting contractions long before Goodwife Reynolds grasped the child—she thought by the shoulder—and pulled it from her body, which ripped and tore.

"Thank our heavenly Father it got as far as it did," Jennet heard her tell one of the attending maids. "I could see the head. Else we should have had to call for the physician, and your lady might not have lasted long enough for that. I believe the cord—that happens sometimes, the cord wraps around the neck."

Jennet heard this all. They must have thought her insensible. She feared the physician with his glittering instruments. She tried to be thankful, though she cried out for grief.

Her breasts hurt terribly, were hard and hot, for days afterward. At least it was winter and there was ice in London, applied as Goodwife Reynolds instructed, but she was in agony just the same, and she lay on her bed and moaned, wondering when, when the pain would go away and leave her be.

Jennet knew that women lost babies, and often. She knew of many women who had lost their first ones and who now had gigantic broods. She could weep for a time, and then she was expected to discuss such things calmly. Every day at least one of her brothers came to see her. They were not the comfort her mother would have been.

Still, after a time, her husband came into her bed again. This made her sad, as it reminded her that this was how they had made their first baby—a boy, they had told her when she was feeling better—but she hid her sadness so as not to upset John. "I am not exactly as I was," she said when he was finished and lay still on her, kissing those breasts that had been so sore.

"Nay, that is a fancy, love," he said. "You are, truly. Still my beautiful Jennet." He did not notice yet, she supposed, that while her body looked almost the same as it did before she was with child, it had lost a sharpness, an adolescent edge that it would never regain. And he could not know that nausea came upon her more easily now than it ever had.

When she knew again that she was with child, her brothers did not bring anything. They were concerned about tempting fate. But she looked at the things they had brought before, far too valuable to be discarded only because her first baby was dead. She knew she still favored the same names, but she refrained from saying them to herself.

"I made the acquaintance of such an interesting man!" John said to her one day at dinner. He had gone to the theater that afternoon, to see *The Spanish Tragedy*, by Kyd. He asked if she wished to join him but she declined—she was afraid of being ill and vomiting in the theater. She still had a hearty appetite, although to actually smell cooking turned her stomach. "One of the young players, from South-wark," her husband said. "I have asked him to dine with us tomorrow."

She only raised an eyebrow at him. She enjoyed enter-tainments—she even wrote some poetry herself sometimes, following the example of the queen for well-educated young women—but players were an uncertain lot.

"He seems very different from most players," John con-tinued, smiling at her, guessing her thoughts. "He is quite a respectable young man. And he writes verse." He thought that might please her.

So many unspoken words in a marriage, thought Jennet. John meant that this young man was not given to excess of drink, did not visit the brothels of Shoreditch and Cheap-side. But he did not think it proper to talk of such things to a woman. He forgot that she was bred in London, that her brothers had roamed the town in that alarming fashion of boys.

He wants me to be amused, as he is leaving again so soon, she thought. He thinks a poet may amuse me. Well, that is so, he may.

"I'm sure I will be very happy to welcome him," she said.

The gentleman came and was quite nondescript. Gray eyed and brown haired and not particularly tall. He did not talk much, only as much as he needed to be polite. John inquired of his wife in Stratford.

"She is well, thank you, sir."

"How often do you see your home, Master Shakespeare?" asked Jennet.

"Not above once a year, madam," he answered.

"That must be difficult."

"It is."

"Difficult for Mistress Shakespeare, as well."

"Yes, madam. But I am fortunate—Anne is excellent and capable in all things."

It is his voice, Jennet thought suddenly. That is why he is not talkative. His vowels resonated with the country, with the Midlands—everyone in the city would know, as soon as he opened his mouth, that he was not one of them.

He loosened his tongue some, however, after her husband's highest-quality Bordeaux, kept for guests.

"I am told by your husband you are a poet, Mistress Davenant," he said after dinner. "Favor us with one of your verses."

"Oh, no, sir. I shall not expose myself to a professional smith of words."

"As you wish, ma'am. I shall not press you," said young Shakespeare, but her husband, also full of Bordeaux, said, "Now, Jennet! Now! Pray do, I have boasted of you and your accomplishments!"

"I will obey, dear husband," she said. And she was

pleased. None ever heard or read her verse but her husband. She went to her writing desk and pulled from it what she thought was her best work. Their guest politely sat up in his chair in an attitude of great interest.

"When I was fair and young then favour graced me;
Of many I was sought their mistress for to be.
But I did scorn them all, and answered them therefore,
Go, go, go, seek some otherwhere,
Importune me no more.

How many weeping eyes I made to pine in woe;
How many sighing hearts I have no skill to show;
Yet I the prouder grew, and answered them therefore,
Go, go, go, seek some otherwhere,
Importune me no more.

Then spake fair Venus' son, that proud victorious boy,
And said, you dainty dame, since that you be so coy,
I will so pluck your plumes that you shall say no more
Go, go, go, seek some otherwhere,
Importune me no more.

When he had spake these words such change grew in
    my breast,
That neither night nor day could I take any rest.
Then, lo! I did repent, that I had said before
Go, go, go, seek some otherwhere,
Importune me no more."

Young Shakespeare applauded, loudly.

"Nay, sir, your appreciation is in the wine," she said.

"Truly not, lady," he answered.

"She draws as well," said John. He motioned to a pair of screens in the room, of her own working.

The young man got up from his seat and considered them carefully before admiring them.

"Lady, they are beautiful," he said. He turned toward her. "Quite a cut above the works of most accomplished ladies."

"I thank you."

"I am sincere now."

And she smiled, and looked down and blushed most charmingly.

John had to voyage for business again, and through the spring Jennet was home. Every day but Sunday she heard the trumpet calls of the theater across the river. She grew quite used to it, thinking of it as company, at two o'clock every day, a notice that all was well and usual. Once the baby was born, she thought, she and John would go again.

Once again her husband was home in plenty of time for the child's arrival. It was a girl. She lived—for a day. John had insisted on a physician this time, but the birth was uncomplicated, he need not have done so, at least for the delivery. The physician liked Jennet, thought her brave and plucky. She tried very hard not to cry out. She had the thought that if she did she would attract the attention of fate, of the universe, and she wanted her child to slip into the world unnoticed, no bother to anyone or any malevolent spirit of destiny.

But the girl died anyway. She was taken with spasms on the second day of her life and died before the physician could get there. And Jennet lay again on her back in bed. Her breasts, which this time had at least nursed, were hard and hot again, and there was no ice in all of London because now it was summer, and the plague was around every corner, and her face was covered with sweat, the veins on it showing red because she had burst them pushing her daughter from her body.

John thought she should get out into the city, again take up her pursuits, write a verse here and there, and find her pencil for drawing, not lie listless in bed. She made an effort when it became cooler and the evenings came earlier. They dined with business associates of his and with her brothers and their families. They watched a procession of the queen's at night by torchlight, as she entered the city again after her summer progress through the country. John took her to the Rose in Shoreditch to see a comedy to cheer her, one called *Love's Labor's Lost*, very silly. Lovesick fools and everyone running around and unsure of who was who and who was where. John paid for extra seats in the high-priced gallery, that she might sit in unusual comfort. After the applause he got up and said something to one of the attendants at the door, an old woman who bowed to him and made a sign that she would return.

"Pray sit here, dearest, until the crush is over," said John, and they stayed as they were while the crowds pushed out.

The doorkeeper, pushing against all those persons going in the opposite direction, reappeared, bringing with her the young theater poet who had been their guest some months before. He was still costumed as Nathaniel, the curate.

"I am so pleased to see you here," he said, with a real smile, quite genuine and broad.

"This was your work, then? Well done!" cried John.

"Thank you, Davenant. I have not seen you these long months. Where have you been?"

"France. For business. Come and sup with us."

He motioned toward his clothes. "I must needs make myself a proper man and not a curate, first." He stole a very quick glance at Jennet. She knew not why. She did not know how beautifully her hair shone against her skin at her brow that day.

"I'll attend my wife home," said John, "and you follow when you can."

"I will."

John took her home quite pleased. "We must talk to him some of poetry," he said. "You enjoyed him, did you not?"

"Yes, sweetheart."

He arrived, they ate supper. The table was more sumptuous than before. John had prospered with his last enterprise. They removed from the dining parlor to the salon, and the gentlemen lit pipes, the newest luxury.

"What think you, sir, of these melees?" asked John. Of late the apprentices had been rioting, accusing the government of failing to protect them against foreigners, some of them French refugees, Protestants fleeing the Papists.

"Shortsighted," said their guest. "The time may come

when they themselves need refuge. Very unstable, these times."

Jennet rose. "Pray excuse me, gentlemen," she said.

"My dear?" asked her husband. "Do we bore you? We may talk of something else."

"No, no, I must simply see to the servants over the wine for after supper," she said. She went to her bedroom and sat on the edge of her bed for a moment. She so wanted to simply be quiet, at home. Not to speak to anyone. Not to be a hostess.

She took in her breath deeply. She rose again. She returned to the salon. She was puzzled to see Shakespeare alone. "Your husband went to see what kept you," he said. She sat down opposite him, moved the hoop for her embroidery before her, and began to work.

He began to say something. He stopped, then began again. His hands had been still in his lap, but now they moved slightly, folded, unfolded. Then he kept them still again.

"Your husband told me of your loss, this recent summer," he said. "I really am most sorry."

"I thank you, sir." She pushed the hoop away from her again, and with her own hands motioned toward her body, toward herself, her torso.

"I am not." She stopped, unsure of what she was not. There was no real word. "I am not what I was before."

His face showed some surprise that she had talked so to him, but he answered calmly enough. "No. Well, you would not be."

John bustled through the door, followed by the servant

with the sweeter wine. "There you are, my dear. Did you never get to the housekeeper? There, you see, we have attended to it all." He poured the wine for all of them, and they drank it, the men quietly conversing on the difficulties the theater business shared with all others, Jennet appearing to listen.

Some four years later she cheerfully called, "Will! How goes it?" outside her door, standing with her delicately shod feet on the solid stones of Maiden Lane. "John is not at home, I am afraid."

"No, no, I am to wait for him here, and we are to go to the Mermaid," he answered.

"Are you dragging my husband to the taverns again?"

"Aye, mistress, shall you come too? Shall you delight my debauched player friends with your bewitching smile?"

"I am a respectable lady, sir, unlike those others you keep company with, and I shall *not* accompany you."

He put his hand to his heart. "It is shattered, lady."

"No more than you deserve."

"How goes it with you, Mistress Davenant?"

"Well."

He looked at her with his face softened. "Truly? Well?"

"Indeed. Well." Now she feigned irritation. "Bring my husband home before dawn and while he can still take off his own boots, if you please."

"Where do you go? Shall I attend you?"

"No, no. I have a simple errand. The maid will attend me, you see. Good day—shall we see you Saturday?"

"Oh, yes. At five o'clock."

He bowed. In four years' acquaintance, he had never touched her. Never even shaken her hand. As was mannerly, for a gentleman and the lady who was his friend's wife.

Her young maid, silent, followed her through the streets of Cheapside until they came to a house not grand but far larger than those beside it on Sailor Street. A porter answered their knock.

"Master Forman expects me," said Jennet. She instructed the maid to wait for her and followed the porter to a landing, on the second floor, outside a solid, dark plank door. He knocked, received a grunt in response, opened the door, showed her in, and left the room, closing the door again behind him.

The office of the learned astrologer Simon Forman was dimly lit—very thick blue velvet drapery kept out much of even the afternoon sun. It was a square corner room, with windows on the two sides facing the street. There seemed to be a writing desk beneath one of the windows, and a man at the desk, sitting with his back to her.

"Mistress Davenant?" said the man, into the window.

"Yes."

The man rose and turned. Jennet's eyes were adjusting to the light. He was not what she had expected—although she was not sure what that was. She had not fancied he would appear like one of the wizards in a treatise on the threat of witchcraft, in a conical hat and a robe covered with strange devices and markings. But she had not thought she would find this neat, bearded gentleman, no older than her husband, in his respectable silk doublet and buckled shoes. The office itself was unremarkable—no golden sparks flew from any of the books on the one wall lined with bookshelves, and the rich Arabian carpet, not unlike some of those that John purchased, did not appear magical. It could have been any prosperous scholar's workroom.

There was one simple chair, other than that at the writing desk. Forman motioned to it. "Pray sit down."

He drew his own chair from the desk to face her, sat, leaned back, placed his fingertips together.

"Your time of birth?" he said.

Patiently, Jennet recited the dates, times, places of birth of herself and her husband. She had not written any of this down to give the astrologer—she had not wanted her husband to find even a scrap of paper, to ask what it was for, to find out that she had come here.

"And your query?"

She did not even wish to say it. It seemed, again, to draw the attention of the fates.

"I have lost five children," she said. "Five. All stillborn, or lived only a few hours." She gulped and continued. "My husband, he had been used to go away, sometimes, to see to his business—he went when I carried the first two. Then he stopped going. But that does not help me. They just come, one after another. I only bear them to die, delivering them up already dead to God. I wish to know, sir. Are we bewitched?"

"What are the dates of birth of the children in question? And the times of day, do you know the times of day?"

Oh, she did. She would always know. The first one, born that hard cold winter afternoon. The next one, that summer morning. The two in April, one at night and one in the morning, a year apart, both in the rain. And finally, the little girl who came hard so close to Christmas Day.

Simon Forman considered. "There is nothing in the chart," he said, as though thinking aloud. "Have you been unfaithful, madam?"

"No!" She stood to leave.

"I do apologize, madam. I do, pray sit again. I must eliminate possibilities, you understand. Pray sit down."

Stiffly, she did. He rose, took down books, considered again, read from two treatises at once, one open on each hand. Finally he said, "The air of London has been poisoned these last few years with humors, madam, humors particularly harmful to a lady born with the sun and moon both in Pisces, as you were. Dry, hot humors. These are lifting, with the transition of Saturn, lord of discipline, into the next sign, and Jupiter entering Pisces. I predict, Mistress Davenant, that the next child you bear will be healthy. The danger should be over."

She wanted to weep, not for sadness or joy but because she had not realized in what tension she had held her body, and how it dissolved as it relaxed, in a moment, and she held it so no more. She paid him his fee. Five pounds in gold. More than many workingmen earned in a year. More than her husband's friend Will Shakespeare earned in a month. Outside the astrologer's door she repeated her admonition to the maid not to tell her husband where she had been, but she walked home lightly, daring to hope.

Midwives said, "Once a babe has lived its second summer and its second winter, it is safe." They meant safe from particular childhood miseries, murdering illnesses, or horrible pestilences that could leave them blind, deaf, or crippled; they might yet certainly die at any time of the same specters that could kill their parents. Still, thought Jennet, more and more coldly, more and more searching for some logic clear as diamonds as to what was killing her babies, they should not have named their sixth child until he had passed his second winter and his second summer. Perhaps they had tempted providence. But it seemed an auspicious name, John, her husband's name, the name of the most beloved of Christ's disciples. They had been so hopeful.

"Five is such a round, final number," she told her husband, trying to explain her optimism, her certainty that this time, this one, would be different. "I cannot believe that God would visit us with this curse yet a sixth time." Even Pharaoh lost only his firstborn. Even the Virgin lost only one child, and she was at least allowed to watch him grow.

She did not wail when this one died.

When he returned from Stratford this time, Shakespeare went to her house first before his own rented room. John was about, but the servant showed Will into the parlor, where Jennet sat at her correspondence.

His hair, she thought, was going, and she was then ashamed of herself for having such a mundane thought. She knew what had befallen him. His only son dead from fever.

"I am so sorry," she said.

"I thank you." He vaunted at a smile, neither she nor he knew why, and gave it up.

"Sit down, Will."

He sat quite quietly, and she called for the servant to fetch John from his office.

There was silence a moment, and then he said, "I am working on something. It does help."

"I am glad of it. What?"

"The tale of the prince of Denmark. Do you know it?"

"I believe I have heard of it. There is a history of Denmark, I believe, with the story?"

He nodded. "My prince," and here he smiled wanly again. "He does not see death as you and I do. To him it is weighted equally with life. Only another place. Simply . . . I do not know . . ."

"An undiscovered country."

"Yes."

"To be or not to be, as if there is almost no difference," she said.

"Yes."

And she was at his feet, weeping. "Your wife," she said. "Your wife. I cannot imagine . . . She has lost her only son. . . . I am so sorry for her, so sorry, you see, oh forgive me, I do not mean to make such a spectacle. . . . She must have watched him breathe his last, how could that have looked? . . . She must have hoped, so hoped it was not true, looked on his face and thought she saw it move, thought she saw a breath. . . . She must have held a looking glass over his face, to see if it fogged. . . . And he will never come to her or you again, never, never, never, never, never . . . your Anne." And it seemed there were not enough tears in all that great city for this man, his dead son, and his wife, the wife of this man who was kissing her. His kisses were on her hair, and on her wet face, and on her mouth, and she was glad of them, and her hands were around his neck. She had never touched his skin, in all these years neither had even put a finger on the other's arm, but now she did, and they heard John upon the stair.

And she was weeping quietly back at her desk over her unwritten letters when her husband entered, so broad shouldered and gray now, so different from what he had been when they first married.

The poet stood, to explain, but John stopped him with a hand. "No need," he said. "No need. I understand. I do not wonder she is upset, to know what has befallen your family. Will, I am so sorry for the loss of your boy, so sorry, I do know. I was so grieved to hear of it." He went to his wife and put his hand on her shoulder, trying to comfort her, and she buried her face in his shirt.

"I am taking her away from here," he said. He looked around at his rich room, the ornaments of gold and silver and glass, the heavy brocade hangings. "I hate this all. London is poison."

John took Jennet to Oxford. They gave it all away, far under price, all their rich goods, to be rid of them quickly, caring only to save enough to purchase the wine tavern near Corn-market. The students and teachers would use it as their common rooms, as they did the other three taverns in the city, and the former wine merchant and his wife would have enough to live on, simply. Families did not then often move from town to town; some young people might leave a village for London, but that was all. Jennet's brothers were concerned, but she assured them this was her wish as well as John's.

"You can stay with us, Will," said John. "On your journeys home each year."

"I will," said his friend.

Jennet's little boy, two years old, ran out the back door of the large four-story building that was the wine tavern. Every room was full of smoke and the arguments of students and masters, save the family rooms at the back, where Jennet and John and young Robert lived and slept.

Will scooped up the little one and covered him with kisses, kiss after kiss, held him tightly, showered him with kisses, a rainfall of kisses. The boy, who could not remember a stranger he had seen only once, a year ago, tried to push away, but Will would not let him go until his mother walked out the same door from which he had come to retrieve him, her husband not far behind.

"He is beautiful," said Will.

He shook hands with John and tried to shake hands with Jennet, but she quickly drew her hand away when she saw what he intended. He looked, then, quickly at her face, and she saw his eyes were hurt. Then she looked at her husband, to see if he had seen; there was no sign he had.

"I have brought him a gift," said Will, waving his hand at their son. He showed them a pair of fine, fine men's riding gloves, tiny, for a small child's hands. "Made by my father. I think it rather amused him to make some, after so long."

Robert crowed and snatched at them. Jennet told him to

mind his manners and greeted Will with warm words. She went to make up his bed, leaving her husband to show his friend about the place, now newly painted in some places, with additions made.

They had a long evening. Jennet waited on some of the tables herself. But deep into the night Will and John drank and talked in the little parlor in the back of the tavern, and finally Jennet lit a rush light and took their guest to the door of his room.

As they climbed the stairs he asked her, in John's hearing as he bolted the doors downstairs, "Have you been drawing? How is your embroidery, your poetry?"

"Oh, I do not have many hours to spare for those things now."

Outside his door he grasped her hand, and this time she allowed it.

"Have you forgotten me, Jennet?"

She did not answer.

"You have."

"No. No! I have turned toward life now. This life. I choose this. I cannot have any part of the other. But I have *not* forgotten you."

"But you do not remember, either. Not as I do." He moved closer to her, and she felt she breathed his own breath, as she had those three years ago the day his mouth moved through her hair.

Selfish, she thought. Men could be selfish without even knowing it, it was such a part of their being. Her own husband, all those years he went away across seas she would never lay her eyes on and left her in his house alone. This man now beside her, his head bent toward hers, his hair and his eyes now both gray and soft, who would not leave her her peace. Who insisted she think of him only as he wanted her to.

"You should behave better," she snapped suddenly. "I will remember as I choose." Then, by way of being more gentle, she said, "I am with child again." And he saw that her face was warm, tinted rose in her happiness.

"Well," he said. "I am glad."

She gripped his hand more warmly once before she withdrew her own, knowing now that they would never touch again. She hoped he knew it too, and, she told herself, she hoped he was without regret.

She opened his door and he went in. She went back down the stairs to help her husband, and then the household was all abed.

Jennet did not feel that after all she had been through she was under any obligation to explain to anyone why she called her second surviving son William. It did not displease her husband, and that was enough for her.

Dark Blue

"I'm going down now," Ophelia said aloud, though she was alone in her room in the great stony castle.

Dark blue her spell was, those weeks ago. Not black magic, no, dark blue, like the water. In the night she burned the iris-colored candle on the bank of the stream at the place where the water pooled. She bought a silk fishing net the shade of the shining algae to spread around the flame. Blue was the color of the water, of the waves of love and the waves of joy.

It is cold in Denmark in the winter. Waiting in the snow beside the iced-over pool tired Ophelia, weakened her joints and made them tremble, gave her face a flushed burn, numbed her hands. There is a tension that begins as soon as a spell is under way, difficult to tolerate for a sensitive girl like Ophelia, whose nerves rose almost to the surface of her skin, buzzing and raw. Before beginning such rituals she had to force herself past an inventive procrastination she always devised. She didn't like to start. Oh wait, she would say, I must first put away this bit of jewelry, this sapphire heart on a gold chain, found out of place here on this table. I must straighten my whole jewel box. I must straighten the whole table. I must first wash my face and hands with salted water, to purify myself before I begin the magical work. I must have a drink of hot wine, for my strength, because I will not be able to stop for anything to sustain me once I have begun. Wait, now I've spilled the wine, I have to rinse away the spill, I have to call the servant to take away the cup and the cloth . . . and so on. And by then the moon has gone void-of-course again, the night is gone, and the spell must be put off.

When Ophelia first began to plan her conjuring she thought of going to one of the professional followers of the old ways; they were still plentiful in the surrounding villages, despite the growing injunctions against them. But in the end she did not. She was concerned about what a spectacle she would be. It was difficult enough to buy the fishnet; she had to send a maid, the youngest and most timid girl she could find, so that she could be sure of at least frightening her into silence, and even then endure a curious stare from the little thing. How could she leave the castle, in a carriage or sleigh or even alone on horseback, without the whole countryside knowing, without her father knowing? A fine lady alone in the middle of winter, a richly dressed young figure out in the eternal twilight of those months, she would be like a bright rose against the snow. And supposing she did manage it—sneaked away in the cold, secretly arrived in one of the villages half frozen? Even if the particular woman she went to were respectful and discreet, still, those women might talk among themselves. And any farmer or merchant might see her, however careful she was, and it would take only one. She was not a princess—as her father had reminded her when he saw the glow in Prince Hamlet's eyes, saw the letters and poems the prince had written her, saw the glittering hard sapphire heart he had sent—but she was the lord chamberlain's daughter. If any little excursion were commented upon, it would get around the country in hours, and her father and possibly even the king and queen would discover it, and she would have to explain, and what was she to say? That she so loved Hamlet that she had gone to a sorceress and cast a love charm on him? Better to do it herself.

She could talk of her love to no living being, no laughing, gossiping friend. There was not a single other young girl at the castle. Her childhood playmates were her brother Laertes and his friends, the other boys—Horatio, Rosencrantz. Not the prince, who was much older and anyway had always been difficult, moody and mercurial, quick to high euphoria or soft sadness. Although he could be witty, too. The tiny band of children of the castle had a private joke with him. When they happened upon him with a book, which they often did, they would ask him, "What are you reading, my lord?"

"Words," he would say. "Words, words, words." He would hold up his page to show them and they would screech, happy. Children love such jests, all the more when they are repeated over and over.

Prince Hamlet was near them all often enough; long ago, when Ophelia could barely walk, he had wrestled with them, carried them two at a time on his shoulders, then still gangly with adolescence, let them win at fencing and races.

She remembered, not long after his kingly father's funeral, unseen by her and talking to the queen, he had suddenly sunk to his knees and buried his face in Gertrude's belly like a child, and his mother had stroked the hair of her tall, strong, mourning son, adult now, thirty years old. Ophelia had seen such a sight before, when he was not yet nineteen—what had happened? She did not remember. He had wept in his mother's lap, and Ophelia, a tiny child, had thought that strange, a big boy crying to his mother, but also somehow natural and in keeping with the prince's ways.

When the boys grew up and went to school or war or sea, to the French and English universities or on merchant voyages, Ophelia was left alone. The older ladies, like the queen, thought her sweet and liked her, but could not know her. Her mother was long dead, and though she sometimes managed to call her up from the pooling water in the stream to speak to her, it was very arduous work and not always effective. Sometimes she saw only a filmy vision that disappeared; sometimes there would be no apparition at all. Sometimes she stayed for hours by the pool in the stream, returning sick and chilled, even in the summer afternoons when the roses and pansies bloomed there and the sun glowed orange, and all for nothing. Ophelia always instinctively knew not to tell anyone—boys, women, queen, or king—of her conjuring.

As she grew her father and brother had the charge of her, and she was Papa's little darling. Every girl's father is said to dote, but Ophelia's really did. When she was seven or eight she suffered greatly from leg cramps in the night, and would wander from her bed in search of Papa. He would rub her legs himself, kneading her twisting calves, but never hard enough. He always feared hurting her. She told him her legs were better before he sent her back to her nurse and her bed, but they weren't really. It was the safety she had craved, the warm arms around her, the gigantic hands.

She never even feared that she had displeased her father. It was impossible, he adored her, she pleased him in everything she did. Except in one particular. A year ago, or perhaps two, he had begun his admonitions that she keep herself chaste and pure of thought, and she was not at all sure that she had done what he asked of her.

He told her to guard herself from men. Even Prince Hamlet. Especially Prince Hamlet. A man of the world like him, showered with privilege, so used to having his own way, was full of tricks. And a prince could not choose where he would for a wife, so the only outcome that could come of any understanding between him and Ophelia was dishonor. At first she had not understood what her father was insinuating, and then as she began to, she came to dread his little asides and hints on the subject. He had not been used to talk to her of such things, and it made her unable to meet his eyes, wishing only to fidget and get away. She did not like to think that her father knew about these matters, especially as they related to her. And as soon as she had convinced herself that it was just her father's way, his particular fuss, the bee in his bonnet, that she need not really pay it much mind, her brother had started in. "If he says he loves you," Laertes told her so many weeks ago before he went away through the snow to the university in Paris, "weigh what loss your honor may sustain, if with too credent ear you listen to his songs. Fear it, Ophelia. Fear it, my dear sister."

But she did not fear it.

How funny, she thought now in her room, with the

spring light full in the window and the herbs growing green outside, that no person wondered if she might welcome, indeed long for, his advances; that her curiosity alone almost overwhelmed her, never mind her body's wishes. He might pressure her, her father and brother had warned; how she had longed to feel his pressure. To think of his hands on her, to want them there; to shiver deep in her lower belly when she thought of him, shirtless, washing in the stream as she had seen him do once, out riding with her brother. To watch the water flow over his back, cool, and wish to be that water, rushing over his skin beneath her own sheets. To want to feel the soft hair of his temples against her neck as he turned his head to kiss it, his mouth half open and slack from delirious desire, desire for her. To see his prick, pale rose, cradle it in her hands, watch it grow, know it grew from her touch alone. To feel the deepest satisfactions by her own hand in the night, and only imagine how they would increase if the weight of his body were on her. To already know exactly how it would feel to have her body straining against his, to want to watch his face when he released himself inside her.

Before she cast her spell Ophelia conjured her mother's spirit and it had warned her against what she was about to undertake. Her mother rose above the surface of the pool, a chain of tiny swimming silver fish ever circling her neck, her hair swirling about her as though she were still in the water, not fair and Danish but dark and elfin, like the people from whom she came, the sharp men and women from the island of ice across the northern sea.

"I would not stop you," she said. "You make your own action. You make your own cause. You make your own effect. That is the way of it. But, daughter, love is a discipline. Nothing can bring it into your life if you have not made yourself ready for it."

But Ophelia knew then that she was ready for Prince Hamlet. Every night she waited, ready.

Her mother continued. "Affecting the hearts and minds of others should be avoided."

"But, ma'am, I only want his love. Isn't that a good thing? I think he may love me already. Where's the harm?"

"You wish to force him to do something."

"Only something I think he wishes to do already. Not force him."

"Then why do you do this at all?"

"To make sure. To be certain. Nothing goes quickly enough. I ache when I think of him. I want him so near, nothing but his arms will take the want away. His arms and legs and . . . everything, ma'am. And I am wild with fear when I think he may never come to me."

"These things work themselves into the witch who begins them. They burrow into the body and mind. They become complicated."

Ophelia sighed. "Everybody knows that, Mother."

The spirit went on. "Are you willing to suffer whatever longings you make him suffer? Whatever desperations? Are you ready for something like that, something like him, in your bed?"

"I know how to perform this," Ophelia said. "I will take care. I'm tired now, Mother. I cannot hold you any longer. Don't be frightened for me."

"Are you ready?"

"Yes, ma'am."

Her mother sank softly into the pool of the stream, by the willow, without splash or ripple.

"There's one thing else," she called as she sank.

"Mother?"

"Your world will not look kindly on you wanting this."

"Ma'am?"

She was gone, and Ophelia was exhausted.

When she was a child, Ophelia's mother had always assured her that she was quite capable of any working she chose to undertake. She had the skill. She had the power. Understanding it was something else. Ophelia was only sixteen when she set the candle on the bank of the pool to burn.

That was when old King Hamlet was still alive, before his young brother Claudius took the throne and the world became crazy. Oh, that night out in the hard, bitter cold on the snowy bank of the brook! There was no night bird, not even an owl. No winter flower, no snowdrop, no thistle bloomed. Some bear grass, dead and colorless, bent down, the tips of the blades frozen in the surface ice. It was not a fit night even for the dark moon to show itself. Only the frozen stars glittered around Ophelia, hung about her in the air like glass ornaments.

Then the prince sent her a letter along with the dark blue heart, a rich, noble gift. He wrote her verses in more letters, signed them "Thine evermore, most dear lady, whilst this machine is to him, Hamlet." It had worked. She felt the thrill of the magic through her. She could do it. *She could make things happen.* She felt as though she had drunk from the liquor they served to the soldiers before battle, she felt invincible, she felt she could swallow the world. She was so happy—and so frightened.

Even as a child toddling about the castle, she had always known that she was not a usual girl, a natural girl as others would have been in other courts in other kingdoms. Secretly lighting candles to cure the illnesses of her brother and her favorite maids, knowing the king's and queen's thoughts and hearts without even trying, hearing the secrets of the servants whispered from the stone of the castle walls. But this was the final proof. She had not known she was *such* a witch, to make a man love.

And yet when the traveling players came to court—such a diversion in the endless night of the winter!—the prince cut at her before her own father. He came into the ballroom, which was gotten up as a makeshift theater, hung about with evergreen and the poisonous mistletoe, the only floral decorations that could be had. He loudly asked to lie in her lap and said to her, "That's a fair thought to lie between maids' legs." Trying to shame her, like boys catcalling in the road. He felt his uncle's lust in himself, perhaps. He hated it, wanted to rip it out, and she made him think of it. Perhaps it was even his own father's lust he felt, and to *that* he certainly would not allow existence. How dare he think his father so very righteous, more virtuous than his mother? His father, who would tell the queen he was sorry for their lovers' quarrel after he struck her with a closed fist. His father, who looked at Ophelia in ways she knew her own papa did not like, for she was hustled out of the hall and to bed when those looks began after the feasting and drinking. At least new King Claudius was well spoken and polite. The queen had had no bruises on her face since they married.

Well, prince Hamlet did *not* shame Ophelia. Her gaze toward him was steady, and that night he turned his steps toward her room.

Ophelia did not wish to go to a nunnery, as Hamlet had once told her to. She wanted the heat of a luxurious, passion-filled bed. She wanted to roll around in it, with steaming red silk sheets and a thousand pillows and him, sweating in the cold of the Denmark night. She called him without words, with only will, to her, in the cold dark. She knew what a sickness such as his could ruin, the creeping paralysis of action, motion, mind. She forgave him his nasty talk that night.

When she opened her door he sank to his knees. His mouth twisted, as though he hurt or feared, and he closed and then opened again his pale blue eyes. She had not expected to see them shine so, glittering damp in the dim torchlight of the passageway with unshed tears, and it shocked her. He put his head on her belly. "We can kiss only," he said, burying his face, then lifting it up so she could hear him. "I swear, I swear, that can be all we do. I will not make any attempt on your honor." She knew that would not be what would happen, she knew that was impossible, that he would slide into her within half an hour, it was inevitable. He did not know that. The only way out was to tell him to go away. She let him in, turned down the warm sheets.

She even knew more or less what to do. Somehow this did not surprise him, although at first he had believed truly that they would only kiss. Of that she was sure, as she could read his thoughts; that kind of thing was like breathing to Ophelia and had never failed her. And then she could read in them that as soon as he touched her he knew as well as she did that there was no escape. And her fine dress for wearing to the evening's entertainment was off, and his fingers were inside her, everywhere, in every little hole he could find. At first she was like the water, flowing and sliding against his back with all her limbs; then he turned toward her and she felt his prick so unbearably stiff between her thighs and he dug the pads of his fingers into her buttocks and pulled her to him. And that was how it happened.

So many things about it amazed her, as she lay afterward feeling the newness of it. She remembered details that could not have been. Oh, magical! Magical! she thought. Did all women have these delicious jumbled-up memories? How could his mouth have suckled her breast the time he took her only from behind? It could not—yet she remembered it. How could he have kissed both nipples at once? How could he have been inside her while she knelt beneath him and sucked him? He could not. Yet she remembered it, and a thousand more things—many hands on her, tongues a dozen places at once. His belly against hers—no, that was real, surely? There was no confusion about the silky feel of that. How wondrous is a man's body, so rough in some places, so smooth in others.

After the prince left, in a shower of kisses, fleet footed so he would not be found there, Ophelia waited for hours for her father's return to wish him good night, softly sitting up in their apartment's entrance hall, her feet bare and cold on the floor. She was already meek and quiet with the beginning of a nervous complaint, though she did not yet call it that, she did not yet call it anything. She already knew her senses were not trustworthy and she wanted the reassurance of her father's arms. But he never came.

Finally she went out into the castle halls to find him, padding across the stones. She heard the marching step of a few men, the cadence of soldiers without the numbers of a platoon, and turned the corner from the main hall to the narrow path that led to the chapel. Bearing down upon her were six men, trying to step quietly but hopelessly unable to, both because they were fully armed and because they were trained, as soldiers are, to step confidently and crisply. They were in a hurry, as well, on a mission of speed and secrecy. They carried on their shoulders a simple wooden slab, an old weather-beaten detached door serving as a funeral bier. Surprised, they tried to stop when they saw her, but they stopped too short and they stepped all into one another, and their burden, intended for a quick and quiet burial, tumbled down, and there before her was the twisted face of her father, no life left in it, which took her some seconds to recognize—death changes something about the features—and when she did she screamed and screamed. One of the soldiers called for the queen's old nurse, as though she were somewhere close and could simply come running, and then realizing that she would not, went in search of her while the others held Ophelia down. She screamed, "A surgeon! Call for a surgeon!" Only one man could bring himself to speak. "A surgeon can do him no good anymore, my lady. That time is over," he said, teeth gritted, pinning her to the floor while she tried to slap him. And the queen's old nurse scurried up to her, and while the soldiers held Ophelia she forced some liquid or other down her throat, which for a time made her dull and dead.

Ophelia's father was truly gone. She knew his was not a spirit she could call as she could her mother's. He was in the cold, cold ground.

And no one would speak to her of him. They only said he had been wounded and died quickly of it. She did not understand what manner of wound, why there had been no search or arrest of the traitor assassin. And her sense of other people's thoughts failed her and offered her nothing.

Many lose a father, as King Claudius had said to the prince; they did not all sink into melancholy madness. Perhaps it was worse if the father were murdered. Perhaps, she wanted to say to Claudius, a son or daughter might feel that with all the strength and power of their youth they should have protected their beloved sires, fought as their champions. Perhaps they would be forever haunted because they did not.

The prince was gone. Not a word to her, after such a night as that.

Her madness began almost ahead of its cause. Ophelia's mind took its first quiet steps into the whirlpool before the prince left, before her father passed so violently from this world. It began when she realized *that she wanted.* Her wanting anything became nonsensical when held up against her world, her room, her father, the stony halls, the dead bear grass, the king and queen. And in the chasm between the two—her wanting something and the rest of the world—there was madness. Which was horrible; when it came upon her, she knew what she was doing, but she could not control her actions, as when a muscle twitches or falls into spasm. Whatever she did seemed perfectly rational and called for at the time. Afterward she knew how odd it was, but could carry no memory of that into the next time she behaved strangely. It was as though she were a ship and the instruments of her navigation were simply off for a given time during the course of the day, referenced against a source that no one else used, with the sea shifting. People, she thought in clearer moments, do not fathom that madness is mundane. The mad do not see yawning mouths of hell when the pages open the great hall doors; instead, they listen to people murmur of nothing outside their bedroom doors and hear in it only evil, only about themselves. They feel their hearts separate from their bodies, pounding mercilessly in their throats. Their nerves jump about for no reason, when all around is quiet; they feel deadly calm in their hearts, soothed, if all that surrounds them is chaos.

Oh, not mad, let me be not mad, she prayed fervently, though to her mother or God the Father or whomever else she knew not.

Her poor brother. This very morning, before the king and queen, when he saw how much she had changed over just the last few weeks, how wild his face had turned! He returned from school abroad, in haste because of the death of their father, and found her waltzing into the throne room and nonsensically handing out imaginary herbs and flowers to the queen and company, lecturing them on the meaning and use of each. She had nothing in her hands, she was just pretending.

"There's rosemary, that's for remembrance," she said. "Pray, love, remember. And there is pansies; that's for thoughts. There's a daisy. I would give you some violets, but they withered all when my father died. They say he made a good end."

She had seemed insensible, but she had seen her brother's eyes. He cried out to the king and queen. "Do you see this? Oh, God!"

Then he advanced upon them, with threats in his face, and neither of them had conscience clear enough to hold their ground.

"Does she not know? Does she not know what you have just confessed to me? How can she not know? Good God, does she not understand?"

"She was not told," answered King Claudius, gathering his composure. "We felt concealment was desirable, for the good of the nation, for the good of *her*. What did you think, boy? That we would let it be known abroad, known to *women*, that the prince of Denmark behaved as a common murderer?"

"Send her away." Laertes turned from them and muttered to his own retinue, who gathered round her and escorted her to her room—she led them all about the castle first. But she heard her brother say, as she parted, to the king and queen, "You will tell me the exact manner of it *now*!"

"Let me be not mad!" she cried out to the captain of the men clustered around her, but he did not answer.

Her brother came to her room later and they sat together on her narrow white bed. Gently, he took her in his arms, but she fidgeted. He tried to explain.

Their father was murdered. Prince Hamlet ran him through.

So her brother told her. After the play, Hamlet had done it. He had not been in her room with her, as she had believed.

At that moment he had been sending his great prince's sword through her father's guts and bones.

So she was mad. There was proof irrefutable. He had not been with her. And it had not been like a dream, no, it was far too hard and solid for that. She could not say it was a dream. It was madness, her night with Prince Hamlet. Now she knew. He was with his mother, in *her* bedroom, not Ophelia's bed. He could not be in two places at once. She held on to that; at least *that* belief was sanity. She wondered if it was a demon who had come to her bed and had her that night.

And her prince, and his bloody heart that she thought might still love her, and his body that she felt still belonged to her, all were gone to England, sent away. Probably he would never return alive, and if he did, what did it matter? Things had already spun so far afield, clockwork and wheels, no stopping them once they had begun their inevitable course, ripples of effect spreading out wider and wider by the tick.

She called across the cold sea to Hamlet, "Angry were you, you prick? Over your father? What about *my* father? What about *me*?" Then she gave it up.

She had not intended to wear the hard sapphire heart this afternoon on her way back to that blue water. But then she decided to.

She knew now what she did not know that night on the bitter cold bank by the pooling water at the willow, that she had engineered his love and all else, all that would bring them together. How could it have occurred to her that she, *she*, not the king, queen, prince, or her father, could direct the course of the affairs not only of the heart but of the earth? Its unforeseen methods and consequences?

He murdered her father, her papa, her dear, overtalkative sire, sometimes bumbling, but always careful of her. And yet she wanted him, and her body thirsted for his. And her mind rent in two.

"I did this," she said aloud. "I did this all."

Enough.

"I'm going down now," Ophelia said again, though she was alone.

And she went. The afternoon was bright and sunny. The icicles were melting. And when she finally sank into the water, what relief. Water washing it all away. Her deeds and the deeds of everyone else. Had she done anything so wrong? Perhaps so. Perhaps not. But sinking felt good, so good. The pain in her lungs became harder, sharper, then unbearable, and she gasped but that only increased it, an iron band tightening around her heart, and she wondered, was she doing the right thing? But then she knew she was. What other route had she, from where she was, but to do this? Who else might she do any violence to but herself? Where else might she live, with all her talents and workings and abilities to affect fate? With whom else might she spend her days but with him whom she still loved, a madman, a fleeing felon, her father's killer?

And so she did this. She suffered gladly. It would be over soon. She would return to the water, which she loved, the dark blue to which she belonged. And then to the forgiving earth.

Mary Mountjoy's Dowry

I do not comprehend how I came to place myself in this situation. Such a complication is quite ludicrous for a man of my age and station in life. I am respected. I am a gentleman. I am old. My fiftieth year is almost upon me.

The post came to the door of New Place a fortnight ago, with this summons signed by the bailiff, interrupting an important financial conference I was having with Quiney, demanding that I undertake a London journey within one month's time. I had thought myself comfortably settled at home. And I find that Belotte claims that even after eight years Mountjoy never gave him his money, his payment for taking that awkward daughter off her father's hands and putting himself in line to inherit the family business.

This is no small irritation. I am engaged in important negotiations with Quiney, trying to settle the terms for the repayment of his debt to me. (He tries to hide the facts, but I suspect he would not have needed the assistance had it not been for his son's misbehavior. Cockfighting—that is where I believe those thirty pounds did go.)

The fine for failing to appear and be deposed is formidable. The fine for willfully misremembering, of course, is higher still. I can rather imagine the family bringing some witness to say I had knowingly spoken falsely, if the testimony is not to their liking. Then I should need to argue my innocence of perjury, and that, even now, may ruin me.

Nevertheless, tomorrow, in my aged state (although my health, thanks be to God, is yet untarnished), I go before the magistrate. I am to be deposed upon events that I was promised would never return to upset me, a mundane matchmaking duty I performed long ago among the wig makers of Silver Street, where I lodged, to placate that strong-minded Mistress Mountjoy, my landlady. How was I to refuse? And I was happy to hear that her gangly daughter was to be well married, that knobby girl who could not walk by a door without bumping into it.

What could I have been thinking?

I have still, thanks be to God, the journal from that portion of my life; Anne has found it after a ten days' search. It is a great safety. I may offer it as some kind of proof, if my truthfulness is questioned, if the exact information is there. I am not yet certain it is, I have not located the entry. But I was keeping accounts and records carefully then, just beginning to be a truly wealthy man, though deficient in cash from cause of all my investments; I put my own money into the theater at Southwark, and New Place in Stratford needed repairs. I kept a log of money spent in one ledger and in another a brief synopsis of all my days. Her Majesty, then, was dead less than a year, and we—the theater men—were all concerned about the future of our profession. As to lodging in a simple wig maker's house, well, I have always been a practical man; there was no reason to waste resources, and it was difficult enough to find any kind of room in London. I maintained the country house, with Anne and the girls, and wandered the city eleven months of the year. It suited me.

I remember I was sympathetic to young Belotte, the apprentice. I was apprenticed once—twice, in fact. Once to my father as a glove maker, and again when I joined Lord Strange's company of players, all those years ago, and fixed my fate. But Master Mountjoy, the wig maker, never did me any harm, either. A bit miserly was he, a bit gruff, not a delicate man, but wry and wise to the world. He did well in London. You would never have known him for a refugee, a Frenchman fleeing Papists.

I am tired. The journey to London is more arduous upon my bones than it once was. I shall review the pertinent entries before my deposition, see again what I may find.

August 27, 1604

Took up lodging in the house of a Master Christopher Mountjoy, one of the score of makers of wigs and ornamental headgear in Silver Street. He is a lean man about my age, with a stout wife and an unmarried daughter about my Susanna's age, or perhaps a bit older, yes, twenty-five or twenty-six. He has a grizzled red-brown beard and seems a shrewd tradesman. Price, six shillings per week, payable every Monday, breakfast, dinner, and supper included. Quite within my means. Neither the house nor the room is particularly large, but they are well constructed. The workroom takes up much of the ground floor, with a comfortable kitchen and family room behind, and a yard outside where is kept poultry, the kitchen garden, and so on. There is a narrow, narrow staircase, with my room, larger than the Mountjoys', on the left; their chamber is to the right. The garret is partitioned with a room for the apprentice and one for the daughter of the house. My own straw-filled bed is comfortable.

Jonson and Burbadge recommended the place to me; they each have lodged with families in this street from time to time. And it is close by Southwark and the Globe, over the water. I should establish a true property of my own here in the town; I should lodge according to my means. But there is such an unholy demand for rooms and houses as the season begins—I was fortunate to get this. For now, it will serve, it will serve.

September 1, 1604

Mistress Mountjoy is a talented cook. As I made my way home early this evening after a meeting I had not expected she would have a dinner waiting for me; beef with mustard, bread, and very good ale. My six shillings are well spent. I was pleased to find something to eat. There are problems with the play—the master of revels in his role as censor objects to Antony's speech, on the grounds it encourages a crowd to riot, and we must alter it to be less incendiary, but then we must still allow it to demonstrate Antony's coming ascendance by popular support. I am quite exhausted.

The meal was served by the Mountjoys' daughter, Mary, an awkward creature if ever I saw one. She is tall, but somehow never seems to take up much of the space in a room unless she is knocking something over. Her knees and elbows are so bony they stick out from her like the spokes of a wheel. It is no wonder she constantly strikes them on this and that—the edge of the open door as she maneuvers past it to the table, the corner of the coal hod as she stoops to place a last bit of fuel on the fire before it dies for the night. She spilled my ale, although only on the table, not my lap; her mother scolded her severely in French. She said not a word I could hear the whole time, but did mouth what looked like "Pray excuse me, sir," when she spilled my tankard.

She does put me in mind a bit of my own Judith. Judith is not so silly, but she is too tall, as well, and often silent. She is dark and sometimes sullen, even to me, her father, when I do see her. Why? I do wish my daughters would marry, and marry well. My position should help them, but there is no sign of a match for either one, and Susanna is already twenty-one and Judith eighteen. They neither of them received their mother's looks—Susanna is fair, but without Anne's warm expression, and Judith, again, though tall, has this high forehead that graces my brow and points up her sullenness all the more, the way she broods with her dark eyes.

Enough, I shall cease rambling. I am tired, I am troubled about Antony's speech. It is cold in this room. Good night, friend journal.

September 10, 1604

This evening, now the nights grow darker all the sooner, I sat at Mountjoy's table and drank an ale with him. We both became rather slurred, but I found I enjoy the man. He lacks higher education; but then, so do I. I take it he has also been something of a favorite with the ladies in his time, although he intimates that Mistress Mountjoy keeps a heavy watch upon him now.

"Now you, Master Shakespeare," he said, "you're a better-looking fellow than I am"—and I am not a vain man, but this I must own as the truth—"and no doubt the ladies flock round you, with that poetic tongue of yours. But I did fair enough in my time. I was amusing, you see, sir. 'A lady is like an otter,' I'd say, to get their attention, and, 'Why?' they'd say, and, 'Because a lady is neither fish nor flesh,' would say I, 'a man knows not where to have her,' and you would think they would take offense but they did not, and as long as I kept it up—so to speak." Here there was a loud chuckle from us both. I do not know what manner of ladies he was keeping company with; but I may certainly not pass judgment there. I am not so circumspect as I was when I was young. Mountjoy went on. "In those years I would have a flock of them hanging about me like doves. Ah, hands like doves, Master Shakespeare, don't they all have hands just like doves?" And here he sighed and placed his head upon the board as though to sleep.

I sighed as well. "They do, Master Mountjoy," I said, and I thought of my little Nell. My little Nell is married now, and I cannot even complain.

She was not the first one with whom I broke vows with my beautiful, soft, far more deserving wife. No, that was a professional at Kenilworth, while I was yet home in Stratford. That was . . . not important. But my Nell, little Nell. She is still in London, but I know not exactly where. I only hope he is good to her. Yes, I do hope that.

September 12, 1604

Forgive me, Lord, I arrived at my rooms very late this evening—in fact, this morning, for the sun is smiling over the town now, glowing along the edges of the roofs.

Mistress Mountjoy, however, is not smiling. I believe she is ill pleased with me. But Master Mountjoy is a grown man, and he seems rather impressed.

"What, master lodger, what brings you home so late?" he called to me from his dining table, where he sat over bread and a large flagon, his breakfast, I believe. "Were you working?"

"Aye," I answered. I confess I was not without cups of my own working upon me. "Working most terrible hard. Going up and down, and up and down, and up and down."

"I take your meaning, sir, I take your meaning," he called out, rather loudly, and I hoped he would not wake either the household or the neighborhood. "And is she young? Is she pretty?"

And there peered through the doorway into the kitchen the solid Mistress Mountjoy, and behind her skirts—and this surprised me, up so late, or perhaps it was so early—her plain tall daughter, not peering, or in fact even looking at her father or myself. Her mother immediately put her hands on the girl's shoulders and firmly turned her about, then patted her back to direct her into the kitchen yard, muttering something. I am sure that through my haze I heard the word "debauch." Also "God-fearing ears."

"God, woman," shouted Master Mountjoy. "It'll do her no harm to hear something of the real world, tied to your apron strings as she is!"

"I have kept your supper for you, sir," said his dignified lady to me, cold as Innocents' Day morning. "Do you care for it now?"

"No, no, I thank you, madam," I answered, and in truth my stomach could not have well dealt with anything of any substance. "I shall to bed." And this I did, hurriedly, under her eye, making my way clumsily up the narrow stair into my room.

"Never you fear!" called her husband after me. "I shall keep you defended from a goodwife's morals! I shall deliver you from being thrown out into the street!" It was not so very witty, but in a state of embarrassment I laughed heartily along with my landlord. I then bumped violently into Mountjoy's young apprentice, Belotte, Christian name Stephen, I believe, who was coming down from his bunk in the attic to begin his work; it was then I realized it was near daybreak.

Well. God's death, I did my landlady no insult! I do not expect her to receive in her Christian home the dear and lovely but altogether unrespectable Luisa. But surely what I do outside of her house is my own affair. I am discreet. I am a healthy man. What could she expect?

Disturbing news this morning. The theaters are to be closed for an uncertain time, by cause of the "civil unrest." The populace has been riotous in several incidents scattered throughout the city. It is said the king will not enter London, although that may be for fear of the plague. I must use the time in composition.

September 17, 1604

Said my landlord to me yesterday evening—we had elected to go about the town together to some taverns I know of—that he is baffled that I can actually think stories up. "How can you do it, Master Shakespeare? Pull something out of nothing?" he asks, seeing before me at the end of the day a stack of written pages. That is not precisely what I do, of course, but I am not sure he would understand the subtle difference. It is flattering, I must admit, this interest in my work. Mountjoy expressed a desire to visit a public house that some men of my profession frequent, and these he met, cap quite in hand and addressing them as "Your Honor." This might have made them contemptuous of him had he not come in with me, and had they not all been really pleasant fellows, Burbadge and Heminges and their cronies. And they are not more immune than I to praise, however unskilled, and consequence. We are all, at our hearts, populists.

"Does your wife understand you, Master Shakespeare?" Mountjoy called to me across a wide table near the end of the evening, his mouth loose and uncertain. The table responded with general laughter and good humor. "I'll wager she does not."

"To my ill fortune, she does," I answered. "All too well." Which is true, except that it is not to my ill fortune. It is not always pleasant to be seen and understood well, and neither adored nor censured, but it is bewitching. Oh, my Anne. That you had a husband better than I. But would you have loved a man better than I? I do not know.

My remark amused the table as well.

I am not clear how I came to find a way home yesterday

night. I suspect my companion's memory is no clearer. Still, it was a rousing evening, a great relief after all our worries. The theaters are to be opened again, now that the weather has turned cooler and the unstable mood of the city abated somewhat, and I have reworked Antony's speech.

September 19, 1604

   Stephen Belotte, Mountjoy's young apprentice, approached me yesterday at dinnertime. I had returned to the house from Southwark, where Burbadge and Philips are in rehearsal for *Measure for Measure,* of which I must say I am proud, and I think justly. I have tried something altogether new in it; it is a comic play, full of disguises and masques, yet with a dark underside, a sinister comment. The atmosphere is one of a nation oppressed, repressed. Anyhow, Belotte came up to me and was quite shy. He washed up his hands from solvents and glue before we sat down to dine, a funny group about the table. Mistress Mountjoy appears to have forgiven me my libertine indiscretion and sits quiet but smiling, her great mass dishing up her incomparable boiled cabbage and beef with mustard. Young Belotte, who seems an industrious, honest boy, sits, of course, at the lowest place. In him I fancy I see parts of myself at such an age—intelligent and eager and longing for better things than to toil as a craftsman's servant. He is neither too forward nor sullenly silent. Awkward Mary is as quiet as ever, never at ease with herself, her elbows drawn in as though she were afraid that to let her bony arms open freely would bring the crockery smashing down about us, which may in truth be the case.

   But I wander with my words. Midway through the meal,

as my landlord and landlady were concerned with some matter between themselves and their daughter had left the table to bring more bread and beer, young Belotte turned to me and said, "I beg your pardon, sir. I wish to tell you, I had the honor to see a play of yours, the story of the emperor Caesar, two days ago."

"Ah!" said I. "I am monstrous glad to hear it! I am delighted to know of any patron. And did you enjoy it?"

"Oh, yes, sir! I told my fellows I was acquainted with the poet, I was acquainted with you; but none would believe me."

"Well, I shall have to attend you one of these times, and then they will see for certain," said I, and the young man's face looked charged with excitement. I am pleased to give such little pleasures to my audience.

To my surprise, long awkward Mary approached me outside after dinner to tell me much the same. "Excuse me, sir," she began, looking down at my knees or her own large toes, I knew not which, "I felt I had to speak to you." Her voice was raised just above a whisper, and I realized I have never heard enough of it to form an opinion of its nature. It carried a lisp on its s, as did my Judith's. My little one had left it behind, however, when she was four or five, except for the brief time following her twin brother's death, when it appeared again for a year or so. This lady had retained hers; also surprising to me was that the tenor of her voice was neither grating nor shrill. I had expected it to be, from her gait and carriage and face.

There was a twitch to her dark eyebrow that I had not marked before.

"Yes, my dear?" I said to her. I was amused, but tried to speak gently. I am no bully, as my little Nell used to remark, with her approval. I have never taken pleasure from dismissing the timid, I can say that, and I am always good to women. In truth, I am. I like them all. I do not wish to lie with them all, but I like them all well.

"I had the honor of being part of the audience at the . . . the performance"—I believe it was a new word to her—"of *The History of Julius Caesar* on Tuesday afternoon last."

"Now, were you! I am happy to hear that! Young Belotte has told me he attended as well."

"Yes, sir, he accompanied me . . . I accompanied him."

"All in a happy family! And was it a pleasant afternoon?"

"Oh, yes, sir! I enjoyed it very much, sir."

"It warms my heart to hear you say so, young lady," I said. She stood there still, eyes down, in precisely the same pose.

"I am right glad of it," I said. Still she stood.

"Is there anything else, young Mistress Mary?"

"No, sir."

"Ah. Well, then. I must return to the playhouse. Our performance is at two, as always. As you know now. Thank you, my dear." I thought I saw her shudder—it was turning cold, and we were outside the side door to the house, by the kitchen, from which the girl's mother's cries exhorting her to the washing up were beginning to issue. "I am glad that you enjoyed our poor play."

She curtsied, eyes never moving, and turned into the house.

Right glad I truly am to have so much evidence of the

universal appeal of my plays, even to a young, unschooled girl and my landlord's apprentice.

Taking the master's daughter to public plays! Ah, well. I was an apprentice myself once—twice.

October 1, 1604

I talked at breakfast with my landlord this morning, and took pains to let him know that I should like to take him out with Burbadge and Heminges again when our time is somewhat more at our disposal. He seemed gratified at the gesture. I certainly have every wish to maintain good terms with him, and be set down a good lodger.

That boy Rice we have for Isabella is quite a coxcomb, unheard of among these youngsters. My Luisa laughs at his preening when she is in bed with me; but he is the prettiest of them all, and we must make do.

October 19, 1604

Mistress Mountjoy appears to have forgiven me entirely for all my venial sins, for she has come to me with a most interesting proposal.

It rained in sheets today, great silver sheets, and its being Sunday, there was no performance. I stayed in my room almost all the day, going out only for a morning walk when the weather cleared for perhaps twenty minutes together, during which time little Mary (as I keep thinking of her, though the poor thing is so wretchedly tall, towering over the truly little Belotte, whom I see at her side more and more) could clear out the bedding and empty the floor of my crumpled pieces of castaway paper. Well, in the middle of the afternoon, the mistress herself instead of her daughter brought up the tray of bread, cheese, and ale, on purpose to see me.

"May I trouble you, Master Shakespeare?" she said. "I have a matter to discuss with you."

Said I, "Of course, Mistress Mountjoy," though I dreaded another raising of the subject of my nocturnal visits to Luisa, which, until the rain set in last night, have been frequent.

But she appeared to think not of that.

"I have a daughter," she began.

"A handsome girl," I broke in. She quietly regarded me, then continued.

"I have a daughter, who I would like to see well married."

"As many mothers would. "

"Aye," said she, appearing impatient, and I resolved to hold my tongue as it did not appear to be working its greatest effect at recommending myself to the lady. She continued.

"Young Stephen Belotte, my husband's honest apprentice, as you know he is, sir, has approached my husband to ask him what portion would be his, what sum of money my husband would give, were he and my daughter to marry."

She paused, and here it seemed best to say, "I see."

"Aye. Now my husband has said he will give him twenty-five pounds if he marries her, and if he does not marry her he swears she shall never cost him one groat."

I did wince at this. Mountjoy is not a delicate man. And I

did think it unlikely he should get the girl, docile enough but without other attractions, off his hands without its costing a groat.

Now it was I who was impatient. I am not interested in household affairs. "I see," I said again. She seemed to wish to say more, and I added, meaning to joke, "And have you a part in this history for me to play, madam?" How I wish I had not said it—although no doubt she did not need my encouragement for what she was about to propose.

"Aye, thank you for coming so quickly to the matter, Master Shakespeare! I did say to my husband, after we agreed to let our room to you, 'Now there, husband, is an honest, straightforward man!'"

I do admit I started back. "I beg your pardon, Mistress Mountjoy?"

"If you would but assure Belotte, sir. Young Stephen. You know my husband's manner, sir. Gruff. He does not always seem open or sincere. He was quite offhand about the matter, as they discussed it."

"And you wish of me what precisely, madam?" How little did I wish to hear of any of this little drama!

She began to talk quite rapidly, no doubt sensing my irritation. "Would you assure our Belotte, when he asks, that my husband will indeed settle on him the twenty-five pounds? As well as some household linen and plate? You are on friendly terms with my husband, and surely you must know that he is not by nature a cheat of a man. . . ."

I know no such thing. "In truth," said I, "I have never seen his actions in such a situation."

"He would not be a cheat, nor a miser," answered my

worthy landlady. "Our young apprentice does admire you, thinks you a most worthy man, and very great. Perhaps you could simply assure him that my husband will give him the twenty-five pounds?"

I sighed. "I am sure that could be done, Mistress Mountjoy, but why should he come to me for such assurance?"

"Oh! As to that, I have already told him that he should go to you to be certain my husband will keep his word."

"Really, madam!"

"He admires you so, Master Shakespeare. As does my husband. And truly it would be a good situation for my daughter."

I did think on poor Mary then. Unmarried past twenty, like my Susanna—although with far clearer cause. Why do my Susanna and Judith continue alone? My Anne was twenty-six when we married, 'tis true, but somehow this is different.

Well, I am irritated with the manner of my landlady's doing of the deed. But certainly I should not mind to help that timid girl, and if she and Belotte can collect enough money to establish their own household, it may do her good to leave this one. It is comfortable enough for me, but her mother and father can offer her no companionship likely to improve her. And surely what hope does she have but this? And what good could be accomplished by my refusing and thus offending my landlady, in this crowded and costly city where I must be, else languish unknown and unpaid in Stratford?

And so I said, "Well, aye, madam, I will help you. Have Master Belotte come to me if he choose. I shall tell him that verily if he marries with your daughter, Mary, your husband will give him twenty-five pounds. Now, is that all? I shall have no further duties in this vein?"

"Oh no, sir. You have my word you will never hear of the subject again."

"That is pleasing to my ear, madam."

And so here I sit, awaiting the footstep and questioning of the young apprentice. I am quite prepared. Let him come on.

October 20, 1604

'Twas not long after I put down my pen last that Belotte approached me. I had gone down to supper, where he already sat over his pint and meat—roasted chickens, quite a treat. My landlady put down the same before me and with a look in my direction withdrew. Young Mary was no doubt outside in the yard, from which I smelled some smoke and heard the sound of her father's voice, sharp, disgruntled over some affair, directed at his wife or daughter, I know not which.

Well, is Master Mountjoy an honest man? I have never heard of him overcharging a customer, as I used to hear tales of in my father's house; my father, despite his debts, himself never stooped so low. I have somewhat stopped dining and drinking with Mountjoy, as the demands of the season have increased the demands upon me to write quickly and with concentration and to spend extended periods of time at the playhouse. My fellow theater men did not find him offensive. He is coarse with his family, aye, but perhaps that is the French way, and I have known many men out of patience with the wives and daughters of their households—it is not right, certainly, but it does not mean a man will not keep his word. I never heard any real harm of my landlord.

Master Belotte looked up at me as I sat down, wiping crumbs from his chin, which was only now beginning to show a lacy pale beard.

"I wonder if I might trouble you, Master Shakespeare," said he to me.

I leaned toward him, eager to finish the business. "I have heard of your situation," I said. "Be assured that Master Mountjoy will indeed settle on you the sum of money he promises with his daughter."

Rather a cloud than a ray of sun passed over his face.

"I thank you, sir." We ate quietly for some minutes and then he said, "I wonder, sir, if I might have another word. 'Twas another thing I wished to ask you about, sir, not my Master Mountjoy."

"Well? What is it?" I did not wish to be quizzed.

"If you please, sir, how did you think of it? To have Brutus be so tormented and unhappy, instead of Caesar, as Caesar was the one murdered, and Brutus his friend? I have never heard the story like that. How did you think of it?"

I had not expected such, though I was pleased, of course, that the young man took an interest in my work. I was, as I often say, a tradesman's apprentice myself once—twice. I answered as best I could.

"I am afraid I cannot take the credit entirely, though I tried to show how torn he became, how much he wanted to do the noblest thing. But it was Plutarch first posited what an honorable man Brutus was, though he killed his friend."

"Plutarch?"

"Yes, my boy, the Greek—"

"I had Greek and Latin at school, sir."

"Ah." I fell silent, chewing.

"So, then, Master Shakespeare, you sometimes have your thoughts on a play coming from elsewhere? From other people?"

"Oh, yes."

"And that is all right?"

"Perfectly all right," I answered sharply. "I flatter myself that I add to them in the retelling, that I make them accessible to all the populace, render the emotions understandable—"

"Oh, yes, sir!" The boy was quite rosy with enthusiasm.

"I am glad to know you think so." I withdrew soon, our supper being finished, and retreated upstairs to the sound of the rain on the roof, which I was going to term infernal, but which is actually rather pleasant, save that it keeps me from Luisa's room. It puts me in mind of my country childhood. The cold rain of autumn meant All Hallows' Eve, and harvest soon to come, and dancing, and Mistress Anne Hathaway so beautiful before she married me. How are my Susanna and my Judith? Will they dance with young men this harvest?

But enough. My office regarding Mistress Mary's dowry is done. Now perhaps the domestic affairs of the household will no longer visit my door.

October 26, 1604

And now it has rained a straight week. When Mary came up to my room to straighten the bedclothes and restore some order today I was obliged to say, "I am afraid you shall have to do your duties with me underfoot, Mistress Mary, for surely I cannot step out."

"Yes, Master Shakespeare," she said, with no change in her dark little demeanor. Yet as I wrote she stood behind me some minutes. That does make my nerves stand upon edge, and so I stopped the motion of my hand. "Can I help you, my dear?" I said.

"Oh, no—please forgive me, sir." And she picked up my crumpled drafts from the floor. That is a habit of mine. She smoothed them and stacked them neatly to carry them down along with the linens to discard. "That is not necessary, my dear," I said, but she acknowledged me with neither look nor word. How odd that in any other woman—any other person—this would seem willful obstinacy, defiance, this refusal to see or hear me, to answer me. Yet in her it seems meek. Ah, but here my fancy runs away with me. Perhaps it *is* a subtle defiance, belied by her timidity of manner. Such a twist, that would be; a feint within a feint within a feint. Delicious ambiguity! I should make use of that. Silence. Silence can be thick with meaning—and all the better to have one's audience debate it. I may perhaps use silence for my Isabella, in her answer to the duke's proposal at the end of the last act. It may speak volumes. Will she obey her lord meekly, or does she stand even then her chaste ground? I shall try it with Burbadge and young John Rice at rehearsal tomorrow. Silence could suit that boy very well.

But I thought not of this as I turned back to my writing and quite suddenly heard the girl exclaim, "Such pretty names, sir!"

"I beg your pardon, my dear?"

"Moth, Cobweb, and Mustardseed, and what was the other? Peaseblossom. Such pretty names. All in the fairy court! I did delight in them. I wonder if I could ever think up such pretty names."

I turned in my chair to her. My bedding was all gathered in her arm and held on her hip, which is broad, despite her bonyness.

"Why, young Mistress Mary! You have been to another of my plays!" We are alternating my old comedy *A Midsummer Night's Dream*, always very well attended, with my *Caesar* and something of Jonson's these three weeks.

She smiled and actually looked up at me.

"Yes, sir."

"Did you go again with your young suitor?"

Now she suddenly looked displeased.

"No, sir." And she seemed angry. "I saved the price of a place to stand myself."

"Yes, of course you did, my dear," said I, puzzled. A lady does not go to the theater unattended, but no doubt this one could manage to do so unnoticed. "Now, the next time you go, you must tell one of the widows who sees to the attendance that you belong to the household where I lodge, and she will take care to direct you to the place with the best view."

This seemed to cheer her, and she said, "I do not know when I shall be able to go again, Master Shakespeare, perhaps not for many months, but I assure you I did have a lovely view."

"Well, I am as ever happy you enjoyed my poor work."

She only nodded, and turned to go through the curtain of my doorway, and down the so-narrow stair, and then she stopped. She turned about again and put her eyes upon me. They were quite large, and brown.

"If I may be so bold, sir," said she.

I smiled. "Yes, Mistress Mary?"

"Your wife . . . does she understand you?"

I was quite surprised. What has this simple girl overheard, and what meaning has her little heart assigned to it?

"Why yes, my dear," said I. "I am very fortunate in my wife."

"I am monstrous glad of it, sir," she said. And she turned to the stair. As she did I said, to make her easy again and perhaps to flatter—I do try to be kind in that way to ladies—"I understand I am to wish you joy, mistress."

She spoke not to me but to the doorway.

"Yes, sir."

"I hear you are to marry young Master Belotte, of this very house. You must be excited and happy."

"Yes, sir," she said. And she went down.

Odd child—although, like my own daughters, she is not a child, she is a woman by age. I wonder if she is perhaps not quite right in her head, or if perhaps she is not oversimple, that is, deficient in basic understanding.

And that, all those years ago, was the end of it. I find no further mention of Mary Mountjoy in my journal. The two young people married at their parish church one day in November. I was not present, I was at the theater. To the best of my knowledge it was an uneventful wedding day and night, and I did not hear more of the matter. They removed from Silver Street to live with a friend of Belotte's, George Wilkins, a young man of my profession. My own Susanna, thanks be to God, was married some three years later; my Judith yet continues alone and quiet. I went home to Stratford for some weeks after the season, then returned to London, and being comfortable enough and not spending much time away from the Globe, I stayed in Silver Street yet another year until Mistress Mountjoy died, when I took new lodgings. Until the bailiff's demands for my memory under threat of my own financial ruin came uninvited to my door, I had not heard any other word of the fate of any member of that household. But the bailiff's notice did come. And thus, here am I. Called upon to testify to my role as an overlarge Cupid in a match made eight years ago between a wig maker's apprentice and his daughter!

Outside the small room at the parish courthouse in the city, where my witness is to be recorded, I met Belotte. He has not aged badly; if anything the years have made him look more boyish. His hairline recedes beyond his forehead, as does mine, but it makes him appear more childlike. He shook my hand.

"What an unfortunate business," I said.

"Yes, sir," he said. "I am sorry to call you away from your affairs. But truly, my master did not pay me the sum. Do you remember, sir? How he promised to give me sixty pounds?"

I said only, "I am sure we are not to discuss the matter in question outside the courtroom." And I smiled to remember how puffed up I became when he approached me to tell me how he liked my play. I could not, in those days, get enough of such flattery. I am calmer now. My work is as good as I can fashion it. I wish it to be heard, and most often it is. As I am old now, I leave it at that.

"No, sir," he answered me. "Pray forgive me, I am sure you are right."

"How is your wife, young Mary?" And I recollected then that she was not so very young even eight years ago.

He shrugged. "Not unwell," he said. "She is an . . . odd creature, as you may remember."

"Indeed." I smiled, curious as to which particular manner he found her odd. He seemed to see my meaning.

"She keeps such strange little objects about," said he.

"Objects? Keepsakes?"

"I hardly know. She keeps—has kept for years—a nail she found lying on its side in the theater, by where she stood when we went to see your history of the emperor Caesar and his friend Brutus. We have seen several of your plays since then, Master Shakespeare, and are always vastly honored to think that we know you. She keeps also a bit of her mother's hair from her comb. And some sheets of your writing, sir, wrinkled and blotted out, that she used to clear from your room. Do you remember? How she would come and order your room of an afternoon? And you would have the crumpled papers all about? She told me of it. She smoothed some of the sheets and kept them. Vastly strange. I should worry she were a witch were she ever to do anything with the things, but she does not, just keeps them and looks at them once in a while."

"Vastly strange!" I answered. I was afraid my face had turned white, for now I knew all, and I saw and wondered. How could I—and I speak not from vanity now, however I did then—how could I, with all my natural gift for sympathy, with all my compassion for human frailty, which allows me to show it before the world again and again, ever gentle, ever understanding, ever allowing the pain even of those most evil; with my eyes so skilled at seeing and setting down detail of action hinting at the great storms within men's and women's hearts; how could I, in my own absorption with myself and my new money and my new fame, not have seen at least a little into the heart of that poor child, sold off to a low bidder? I did not know. I did not see.

Well, I will not add to her humiliation. I will not be party again to her sale. And young Belotte wants me to say it was sixty pounds, and old Mountjoy, no doubt, sixty shillings. And I remember right well what it was. Yet I shall not say a word. I shall not join in while they quibble over what she was worth. I can do her that kindness, she who understood me too well, she who wondered if she could invent names and verses. She who loved me.

Duty

We heard the running in the streets, we heard the name "Romeo!" called out, but not "Juliet." We had no reason to think Juliet. We knew nothing of what had happened, we thought our daughter already dead. But then we found ourselves summoned, not by servants but by armed men, come from the prince. We were sent for, my husband and I, to come to the opening of our tomb, the tomb of our family, the great yawning maw of death. It had been newly fed.

When we came we found the stone rolled away, like that which covered Our Savior's grave. Now I stand over the bodies of my girl and my enemy's boy, here in the dusty crypt. They are coiled like pale snakes, young serpents of death, he contorted more awfully, by cause of the poison. She stabbed herself instead, made a dagger's sheath of her white untouched breasts. No, not untouched, it seems now. Not quite. And her earlier death was a pretense, to get her to this place and away from us.

The chamber is lined with gloomy stones, the skeletons are faded, gray, common in the sickly light of day that feebly shines—if "shine" is the word could be used for it—through the opening. My nephew Tybalt is over there, a few feet off, green and stinking on his bier, dead three days ago. Crumpled beside him is that fool Paris, who no less than Romeo died for love of my daughter. And I stand and look across the children, across all these pallets of the dead, adorned with jewels, flowers still fresh around Juliet, kept so in the cool of this underground place. I stare across them at Romeo's father, Montague.

'Tis not only ourselves, the bereaved parents, my husband and I and *his* father and mother, about the tomb now. The county Paris's page, the wretched boy Romeo's attendant Balthasar, the old friar, the prince, Nurse—all are clustered here. And outside the entrance, so short a time ago closed off by the great stone, there gather peasants, working men, merchants, beggars in rags, courtesans, and prostitutes, all the city. The day will not be bright, we feel that even now, the dawn so gray and stale, not fresh and cool as a dawn should be. No breezy wind and yet no heat. A still, dead dawn.

My daughter is pale. When she was alive I wondered if she was afflicted with the greensickness, that odd anemic draining of the blood from the face that makes girls her age often so white, with no roses in their skins. I was not so afflicted myself, though many of my sisters and cousins were so. I was, I fear, not sympathetic to their weakness, flushed and strong as I always was, their faces white as tallow.

Now I know she could not have been ill in that kind. I had not seen pale until I saw this face before me; in life she was a red rose compared with this creature drained of blood, all the blood of her body warm on these disgusting stones, running in rivulets between them, dyeing the mortar, the source of the river the sharp little dagger still in her left breast. *He* does not bleed, though he is twisted about horribly, his face an ugly contortion of death, one side of his mouth high in a kind of crooked smile, his fingers held up, bent backward and stiff before his eyes, as though he wished to obscure those orbs from our sight but could not succeed before the last convulsion seized him.

Mistress Montague—I do beg pardon, *Lady* Montague— is about to faint. Not I. I do not succumb to the female weakness of fear of blood, or of the dead. But she cries out to her husband, who stands, it seems, amazed, without comprehension or action. Clouds pass over the faint sun outside, and the light is for a moment yet more gray.

And it is very strange, to be watching so closely the clouds and the light outside the tomb at this moment, and I am sure if I were more foolish I would wonder if I were heartless. Perhaps I do wonder yet. How strange, to watch myself watch the clouds and the light, to feel so very much abroad from here where I am, so removed that I watch myself *watching myself* watch the clouds and the light this morning, while my own girl, my own little poppet, my bean, as she once was within me, lies here curled at my feet, curled around *him*, for *that*, that boy. Oh, she was too young to know there is little more useless than a boy! I did not so succumb to such foolishness, I did *not*; when my turn came, I held my head high, I gathered my strength, I performed the duty required of me, the duty that was best for all, for me, even now. I know this.

How was the stone at the door of the tomb rolled away? I suppose that boy wrenched it aside with the strength of his doomed love. Boys. No boy ever did any such thing for me, despite my beauty. I am still beautiful. I am twenty-seven. I was only a year older than she is—was—now when my old husband, Capulet, and I conceived her. The boy's father, Montague, is yet only thirty. He may have another son, if he has none already, sitting in some harlot's lap. He is not old. Not gray and cantankerous, like my husband. Who smells of decay. Like this tomb.

She has no age now, I suppose, my daughter. My bean.

We have been waiting for the prince to speak first. He carries in his hand a letter, the red seal of which he breaks, and then begins.

"Here he writes that he did buy poison of a poor apothecary, and therewithal came to this vault to die and lie with Juliet."

We know it all. We heard it shouted among the crowd in the streets as we came, despite the rhythmic metal steps of our escorts. "Romeo is dead!" "Juliet did love him!" "They lie now in each other's arms in the tomb in the churchyard!" "She was not truly dead yesterday! Did you hear?" "They were married and none knew!" How do such things creep so quickly, like the plague, into the common knowledge of the city?

Yet the prince would have none but himself give the story authority. He would officiate at it. He further reads the note, the confession of the mortal sin of suicide, left by that boy to his father confessor, Friar Lawrence. The friar nods sagely, as though he knows something, as though he can build for us from this fleshy, deadly crypt some sense and order. But he cannot. Who could build such things, with three boys and a girl slimy with death arranged about us? Order? Cause? Effect? He deludes himself with his own importance.

The friar speaks. "Romeo, there, was husband to that Juliet, and she, there dead, that Romeo's faithful wife. I married them."

Why? How dare he marry children against what he knew would be the wishes of their parents! He's to blame, *I* know, however history may hold it, however gently the prince looks on him now.

"How came your master here?" His Grace requests of poor Paris's page. "To duel with Romeo Montague and die, before this pair then took their own lives?"

The servant stutters, a simpleton, addressed by so great a personage, then manages, "He came with flowers to strew his lady's grave, and bid me stand aloof, and so I did."

Oh, Paris. Milksop. Even as she rejected him in death, he was slave to my daughter's beauty, which was not fine or perfect but simply youthful. Paris, you tadpole, you eunuch.

Nurse is babbling, telling all, hysterical. "You were too hot!" she screams at my husband, as I did when Juliet refused to marry the county Paris, only the day before yesterday—though I was enraged with my daughter, no less than my husband was. How was I to know the fool had already surrendered the prize to this callow boy, this stepped-upon worm at my feet? Yet my lord threatened to turn her from the house, and that I would have no woman suffer. Now with Nurse and all the company, I turn accusing eyes upon my husband, old Lord Capulet. His nose so long, his hair so thin and falling about his ears. He had no time to dress, his doublet is on over his nightshirt, his legs are scrawny and goatlike, though his stomach bulges. Tears quiver over the end of his nose. Regret. Can it be that my hot-blooded lord and master feels regret? I have no mercy on him. There, do you see? I say with my accusing eyes. 'Twas his doing, all his and his men's fancies and prides, his men's contests fought with the size of their pricks.

But Nurse turns on me. She nursed me, too, when she was but a girl and I but three weeks old, and yet she turns on me. "God in heaven bless her!" she cries, spittle on her purple face, waving her arms above my blood-drained daughter. Her own daughter dead, she poured all herself into mine. What a creature. "You were to blame, my lady, to rate her so!" Well.

She turns to the prince. "I tried, Your Grace, to defend her from the second marriage, unholy as it was." Liar. "And my lady told her, 'Talk not to me, for I'll not speak a word. Do as thou wilt, for I have done with thee.' Oh, how could a mother?"

I see the repulsed stares turn toward me. Simperers. It is unexpected in a mother? But yet not in a father? I did what must be done. What else was I to do? 'Twas her father's word was law, not mine.

Yet Nurse babbles on. "Cold, cold mother. My lamb, she was a faithful wife!" she screams, and throws herself upon her. The prince's men drag her away as she screams, and there is an awkward moment as they push her through the narrow opening, out into the street and the crowd. We hear her screams continue, though they fade, and are finally drowned by the steps, the clinks, of her guardians.

Friar Lawrence, now, must have his say. He whirls upon me and my husband. "You!"

"Good Father?" I answer. I am calm. I answer with dignity.

"You betrothed and would have married her perforce to county Paris! Then she comes to me." He gulps air and turns to the little group about us, his hand outstretched to point me out. "And you called for the death of Romeo when he killed your hot-blooded kinsman! Are you content, blood-thirsty woman? *Are* you a woman? Unnatural creature!"

A man, a *eunuch*, to judge a mother! How dare he! When in old Sparta a prisoner of war was to be executed, was it not to their women that he was handed? Was it not their women who tore him to bits? "Unnatural creature," indeed!

And cold, am I? "Do as thou wilt, for I have done with thee." So I did say. And had her father not already spoken? I was merciful, quick, as I hear are the mothers in that far-off savage land of legend, Tchin, where they must by law break their daughter's feet, to keep them small as a child's forever. Best for young Juliet to close her eyes and get it done with, the thing accomplished, go to the wedding as though one were a guest, get to the church, only go, no need to think, allow yourself to be dressed by your maids beforehand as though only for a feast, as I did when I was married to this old man. It is like saying one's rosary, simply making the mouth and body move, no need to hold the thoughts in your mind as you do what you do. The things you need do are most often simple enough. So I would have told her on her wedding morning, had I been given the chance. I knew that in the end such a course would be easiest for her.

I did not know, of course, about *his* son. Montague's. I confess I see why my daughter had a preference. Paris is— was—milk toast, certainly. Here he lies now, dead at our feet, not even a good hand with a rapier. He is smaller and paler than, and defeated by, that son of the handsome, broad-chested Montague, Montague who is so close to me now that if I put out my hand I could lay it upon his round arm. He meets my eyes across the bodies of the dead children. All here do look on me now, but he does not appear to hear the friar's insults. He thinks, perhaps, on something else. His own white nightshirt only partially covers his shoulders, hard and firm as they are, and sharp and yet youthful. His jewels are about his neck, his dressing gown shimmering red and green and gold—he was perhaps on his way to bed, not freshly roused out of it. Yet he breaks his look from mine to whisper to the stained red stones we tread upon, where lies his son. He whispers, "What manners is in this, to press before thy father to a grave?" Any might take him for a loving family man, not one who is less in his own bed than a courtesan's, which is what he is. He who left his son to wander the city unchecked and encounter my daughter.

I make no sound. I am the highest-ranking woman in Verona, the highest-ranking personage after the prince and my husband, and though the friar may rant, none other dare do me any open disrespect. My neck is straight. My eyes are level.

Juliet, child, wretched fool! Paris would have been grateful to her for being beautiful, would have petted and worshiped her. I said I would she were wedded to her grave when she refused him, and so she is. Why under heaven would she believe she might marry where she would, an unsuitable boy? Who told her such a thing? Not I. I was far too mindful a mother. How could she? Well, she has found her deserved punishment. May she revel in it. She has paid for her one night with her love, a thing I never had, a thing I was denied, denied *myself*, and what harm would it have done me? None might ever have known. I know now there are ways to pretend upon a wedding night, not much blood is needed on the sheet, really, that and a cry of pain and no husband would ever have known he was not the first to trespass. It can be managed oh, so easily, but then I knew not, I was too young, I thought all would find out, it would be apparent on my face, that my mother would see. Ha! I never saw with this wench, this strumpet, rolling about in a bed of luxury with her object of lust, Montague's broad-shouldered son. I could not tell with her!

I stare at Montague. He feels it, brings his eyes back to mine. My heart softens, only a moment, as I see the anguish. Only a moment.

"Do you remember?" I say. That is all, but he knows what I mean. All those about us think I am merely cruelly taunting him, reminding him of when his son yet lived, and sharpen their sneers at me. My husband reaches across the bodies to him, they grip each other's right arms, they kiss, they embrace. They vow statues of these children raised in pure gold, peace evermore. None consult *me*. None ask if *I* want peace evermore. I watch Montague's white shirt falling over the soft, curling dark hair of his chest.

He knows that I ask if he remembers the night fourteen years ago of my father's Christmas revels. The night I pushed him away, pushed away his warm kisses in the cold, silent garden, his hands hot on me. The night long ago when I knew nothing. I thought my worth was in my worth to my family. Soiled, I had no price.

Him I loved. Him I did not marry.

No Cause

From Judith Shakespeare to William Shakespeare

My dear sir:

I beg to send my sincere acknowledgments for your letter, which I have just had the honor to receive. I am much concerned that there was anything in my last note to distress you. I must confess I am at a loss as to how I could have been so unfortunate as to cause such offense to you, sir, and I hasten to assure you that it was perfectly unintentional. I am sure news of the kind contained in my last letter to you was designed to bring you pleasure. Indeed, sir, if you will excuse me, I have never heard of a father being made so unhappy, as you have left me no doubt you are, by such intelligence. I rather hoped for an expression of happiness and perhaps, Father, if I may be so bold, of relief.

You know that I have been much alone since Susanna left our house. I only meant to tell you that I was gladdened to have a pleasant companion to keep company with.

Pray let me know by what particular means I have so displeased you, and the why of it.

My paper reminds me to conclude. My mother, in answer to your query, is in good health after her chill, and bids me thank you for your concern, and my sister, Susanna, asks me to inform you that she has not yet located the manuscript that you believe you left at her home before your departure last month from Stratford.

I am, sir, your ever-dutiful daughter,

J. S.

From William Shakespeare to Judith Shakespeare

My dear Judith:

I know that young ladies do not often appreciate the advice of relatives, even of a most devoted father, in matters of the heart. I shall dispense, however, with niceties and insinuation; let me say, my dear Judith, that I have always found you a very good girl, and I know your mother has found you so as well. You are not, perhaps, so fond of society as your sister, but we know you have always been obedient and mindful of what was due your family and parents, and very quick and well witted. It is only natural that the thoughts of a young lady of your age should begin to turn toward concern for her future, to a desire to be well settled and well married, and that she should encourage the company of eligible gentleman. Perhaps it is for this reason that you feel the surprise you indicate in your last note to me, at my distress. But here I appeal, my dear, to that intelligence which I have mentioned. Indeed you may wonder, but surely, daughter, the cause of my distress cannot be so astonishing as you profess.

That gentleman, Judith (and my pen sticks to call him by the term). I think only of your health and happiness; only think on the same, my dear! What are you about?

You mentioned only that you have been consistently keeping company with him, that he has been to the house to see you a number of times; is this indeed the extent of your relationship? Perhaps in my last letter I was indeed too severe. I hope, my dear, that you will allow for a father's anxiety. If you can give me assurance that the young man is no more than a caller to the house, and one of several admirers with whom my daughter amuses herself with pleasant conversation, and that you have formed no particular understanding with him, you will have restored me to happiness.

I am, etc.

William Shakespeare

From William Shakespeare to Susanna Hall

My dear daughter:

Please accept my inquiries into your health and that of your husband and child. I sincerely hope you are all well, and please convey my regards to your husband, John.

London is much the same as always. One would think it would stink a bit less in the winter, without the blazing heat, but a scent of mildew rises from the wet stones that make up streets and lie beneath flooring, and the water in the streets runs nowhere, but stays still and dank and works all throughways into mud.

My lodging, though, is comfortable this season, and we are pleased that it is His Majesty's and the lord mayor's pleasure both that the theaters be open at this time.

Would you be so good, my dear, as to read the whole of this letter, but particularly the remainder, to your mother? I have some concerns I am in hopes of gaining her opinion upon, concerning, as you will soon know, your younger sister.

I am told by Judith that young Thomas Quiney has been keeping company with her. She wrote me this herself, some missive or two ago. You can imagine my response. Young Thomas's father, to be sure, was an honest Christian man; as you know, when he was alderman and bailiff he was a particular friend and business associate of mine, and I was grieved to hear in London of his death. Nevertheless, I am not certain he was the most steady of businessmen; you will remember that some time ago I had the occasion to lend him quite a substantial sum of money, thirty pounds, to help him out of a difficulty brought about by poor planning. Well, I will not belabor that; 'tis true it could happen to anyone; my own father, you will recall, my dear Anne, my dear Susanna, was not always to be kept out of similar scrapes. But his son, Anne! You know as well as I he is a bad piece of work; he had not eighteen years before he was known about town for his gaming debts, from cards and dice and cockfighting; he has been called for reprobation before the church council more than once, and once for fornicating, and all that by his twentieth year. He spends his family's money like water, takes no care with the company he keeps, consorting with servants and worse; he is as often to be found of a morning asleep in a ditch at the roadside from his excesses of drink as in his own bed.

I am told he is of pleasant countenance, that he makes himself agreeable to ladies; but forgive me, my dear, if I do not wholly suspect that his forming any attachment to our Judith has more to do with the portion she has to give in marriage than with any attractions to her personal charms. Judith has never been vivacious, never been what young men on the whole consider lovely, and though we, her parents, find her beautiful, we cannot be blind to this.

I speak harshly, perhaps, my love; I sound cruel, but I mean to be kind; I wish to lay forth bare facts to ensure that our daughter is not taken advantage of. I am sure there are other young men in Stratford, more steady, more worthy, who could be prevailed upon to pay her some attentions, with a view toward honorable marriage. Young Barnabas Tanner, perhaps, or his cousin, that honest farmer Robert Woolsey? She does have that portion to be given, and she is an accomplished housekeeper. Perhaps even an older gentleman, if you know of one eligible, may see those advantages where a younger one does not.

Can you, my dearest Anne, with advantage over me of proximity to our daughter, do something, anything, to detach her from Quiney? If not you, perhaps her uncle, your brother Bartholomew? My love, do answer quickly, through Susanna, and tell me your opinion on all of this.

Your loving husband (and father, Susanna),

W. S.

From Susanna Hall to William Shakespeare

My dear father,

I thank you for your inquiries after our health, and assure you that we are all quite well, and that my husband most respectfully returns your regards. I am pleased to hear that the city, if no better than your usual report, is at least no worse; indeed, I wonder that you can have spent such a portion of your life in it, instead of here in the calmer, greener place of Stratford. I always feel for you, sir, when you write of it. It sounds most unpleasant and trying, and certainly we are all grateful to you for having such attention to our happiness that you submit to spending such an amount of time there.

My mother desires me to take down her words in this letter and to send them to you, and so I shall. The letter that follows is hers, though the pen be mine. I am, sir, your most respectful and dutiful daughter,

Susanna Hall

My very dear husband,

Your concerns regarding our daughter's admirer and her allowing of his attentions are not without foundation, I do acknowledge, but I am not certain the situation is so dire as you imagine, my dear. I think I can safely tell you that situation's cause. Perhaps it is not such as we would all like to hear: surely you must see that she is at the present time without other attractive options. I think, my dear, that so far away from us you carry a lovely picture of a youthful daughter, as well you should and it does you credit. But can you recall that Judith is nearly thirty years old? She has—and this would be, of course, impossible for you to know, since your business through no fault of yours keeps you so far away for such periods of time—all but given up hope. Robert Woolsey and Barnabas Tanner, whom you suggest, my dear Will, are no longer in a position to be prevailed upon to make a match with Judith. The one married Alice Moore last year, and the other has gone to Snitterfield, to pursue a trade in weaving with his mother's brother. Young Mark Smith I might have suggested myself some years ago; as a childhood playmate he and Judith were close. But he died last year of the influenza, have you forgotten?

So I return, my dear, to acknowledging that you are concerned, as am I, but truly I am not sure what my opinion is on this matter. And I confess to you, I know not whether to rejoice or feel some anxiety. It is possible young Thomas is not so very bad. I am no simpleton in these matters, as you yourself will no doubt vouch, and we both know that sometimes one or two indiscretions will grow in the blink of an eye into a reputation never to be escaped, however puffed up may be the gossip. Some information may soften your worries. First, though it is obvious to all that Margaret Wheeler is with child (that cannot be hid), there is yet no real proof that this is Thomas Quiney's doing. Perhaps it is not. Second, some reports, I believe, are exaggerated—sure I never heard of Quiney sleeping in a ditch, and I do not believe he was ever found of a morning in one. Among other reasons, he would pay far too much attention to his own comfort to pass such a night—I am sure he would somehow wend his way to his mother's house and a warm soft bed, the maids and boys there to take off his boots.

No, my husband, I do not like him much, but Judith likes him immensely well. She has had no other admirers, never; you know how she has been all her life— perhaps not all her life. Perhaps only since the death of her brother; it is so difficult for me to remember her person, her attributes, her pursuits before then. All things seem to date from that day. But now, she is flushed with pleasure to have even one suitor, and though we do not perhaps hold him in the highest esteem, he is quite handsome, and many young ladies do esteem him and his smooth voice and easy compliments. He has a way, my dear, not unlike that which you had—though, of course, he is otherwise quite unlike you—of making one feel that he is listening and speaking specially only to oneself, with very pretty words, well turned.

Perhaps he is a forerunner, something of a practice for our daughter. He may "break the ice," as they say, teach Judith what she is about, and others may follow. Otherwise, I really do feel some anxiety for her future. What shall she do, when you and I are gone, if she is an old spinster? It is true you have made certain she shall not want for the means to care for herself (and you must not think her or me ungrateful for that), but what will be her connections to friends in the village and in Shottery? What society shall she keep? How shall she occupy herself? You know she has not the power to make herself charming in that surface way required to be wanted at a dinner or in a parlor, especially as an extra woman, and an older one at that.

So, in all, husband, it may be that this is not a bad thing. And she has not formed any understanding with him. Perhaps all will be well. I shall endeavor to find and encourage other eligible men to visit us. I am, as you know, known to keep a comfortable house and table, and as you say she has some small portion to offer in marriage. Often where one gentleman goes, others will follow. As you suggest, mayhap someone else will step forward. Let us see what will come of that.

Your loving wife,

A. S.

From Judith Shakespeare to William Shakespeare

Dear sir:

I know not what idle tales have reached your ears in the city. Of course, your worries come from fatherly concern for me, but I promise you that Mr. Quiney has explained himself and his part in any indiscretions to me most honestly and in a way that does much good credit on his account. I shall tell you of it, sir, that your heart may be as easy as is mine.

First, last Saturday when Mr. Quiney came to call, though, of course, my mother and the housekeeper, you remember Mistress Quickly, were by, he endeavored to speak to me for a time in relative privacy at the window seat, and took it upon himself to begin the subject of his reputation, which alone I believe speaks well of him.

"I know," he began, "that I am not in general supposed to have behaved in my youth as I should have. I was overindulged, Mistress Shakespeare, and had not the strength of character to rein myself in where my father would not. I am not sure what boy would, but to be sure it has been expected of me by Stratford, and I admit I have failed. It is only lately"—and here, Father, he looked at me most meaningfully—"that I have seen what youthful carousing may have cost me."

He went on to explain that as to the indelicate matter of Mistress Wheeler, that young lady is well known to be lacking in virtue, and that there were several young men in the village—he named them, sir, though

I would not trouble your thoughts with such unpleasant business—who might well be responsible for her
condition. As to his gaming debts and the matters that
brought him before the church council, he admitted of
his guilt in them, which I thought most forthright,
Father, and convinced me of the truth of the rest of
what he said. However, he did also say that he had not
transgressed in any such way these many months past,
and you yourself must own, sir, that it has been several
years since he has been called to answer before the
council.

His final speech went thus:

"My dear Mistress Shakespeare," he said to me, "I
have no doubt that as I begin a new life with a settled
and virtuous woman, one who can and will assist me as
I set my feet upon a path less dissipated, I shall be able
to continue in this nobler vein."

Well, Father? Does this not relieve you? I sincerely
hope it will, sir. I have, you see, no other suitor; it
would pain me greatly to know that this one admirer is
a man who so displeases you.

Your most obedient daughter,

Judith Shakespeare

From Susanna Hall to Judith Shakespeare

My dearest sister,

I send this note via the maid's boy, Percy, who is also
bringing the play that father lost at our house; please

be sure it is sent to him, and do give little Percy a ha'penny, as he has been a most willing helper.

Mother and Father know nothing of your secret. Father is perhaps more displeased than Mother, but I must warn you that Mother is also not happy with your situation, so far as she knows it.

My dear sister, I must add my voice, however unasked, to this chorus of advice givers. It may be that Thomas Quiney will make you happy. I hope he shall.

I know you have longed for companionship—do you remember how lonely you were after our brother died, how you used to speak to him as though he were there, and tell Mother of his goings-on? She was so worried at the time—I remember after many months of hoping it would stop, she finally dictated to me a letter to Father—but I knew, it made perfect sense to me, dear sister. And I am sensible that I left you alone when I married John and came to live in his house. Thomas is certainly very charming, I can see why you are not immune to him. How could anyone be when he smiles with his soft eyes and kisses a hand most delightfully, declaring so openly how pleased he is at a chance meeting? He is nevertheless unsteady, forgive me for saying so, my dear sister, frail in his newfound scruples. Perhaps he will change for you, as you have told me he says he will, and take his business of wine trading with gravity and seriousness, as he ought. That would be a good thing.

But if you have any doubt of that, please do say so, my dear Judith. If you wish for Thomas because there is no one else at the moment, tell me. I could help you make yourself more attractive, to draw other gentlemen. A change to your hair, softer colors of collar, worn near your face, and more important, something of the art of conversation—I could show you these things, and you may feel, indeed, after you have learned them that you have other options.

You know I am a practical woman, sister. When I entered into my engagement with John, I had a real affection and regard for him, as I yet do. He is a good and charming man. Yet it was a considered choice. He is a steady man who is assured, by virtue of his profession of physician, a position in the town, a house, and some property. I would wish the same for you, if it is possible.

Do not mind our father's distress. This is perhaps a thought of a disobedient sort and does not please God, but Father has never known the details of our affairs here and I do not believe he is so immediately made qualified to direct them. Mother has always dealt with events in Stratford, and she is far more sympathetic to your situation.

You do not remember Father before he left, but I do. He put the greatest trust in Mother's opinions and counsel even then. I pray you, however, Judith, do not believe he does not have affection for you. In your note to me you spoke of his being distressed over imagined damage to his name, rather than concern over your happiness and the man on whom it would depend, but I cannot believe him so cold as that. If you had any memory of the time before he left—I believe he adored you, dear Judith. You were so tiny, such a little mop of a thing. He used to pick you up and whisper poetry that you could not possibly understand into your ear. Young Hamnet he bounced up and down, as one would with a boy. But not you. For you there was verse. You know I believe our father knew more of little girls than boys, knew more of how to cheer them. Our brother I do not remember him ever being comfortable with— but then, I may remember wrongly. I was very small myself.

It is no wonder, then, that you do not remember at all. He was barely at home after you and Hamnet had turned two.

My concern, at all events, is not your obedience to our father. My concern is for you. If you are unsure of your happy future with Quiney, let me help you. You and I together may bring about other choices for you. But one word from you will silence me on the subject forever. If you tell me that with Quiney lies your choice and happiness, I will gladly sew your nuptial gown.

Yours ever,
Susanna

From Judith Shakespeare to Susanna Hall

My dear sister,

Indeed you are very kind, but I entreat you do not

imagine that I am in want of help. I am perfectly content.

I believe my situation is difficult for you to understand, dear Susanna. You were always so lovely. There, that is it in its nutshell: you were always so lovely. Your height and fair willowlike appearance were so often commented upon, when we were both yet unmarried. I have been, I hope, not unhappy, finding as I have my own talents in housewifery and the needle, in the other domestic arts, and in reading perhaps more than other women. But your situation and mine in life cannot be compared. I cannot even be compared with our mother. You know how the town still talks of her, still remembers her May Day dances.

Therefore, my dear sister, do not take it amiss if I tell you that I need no lessons in hairdressing, or advice in the art of conversation. I believe I will marry Thomas Quiney, sister, and truly, what should hinder it? Not our father. Small chance he stands, to insert himself in the affair, all the way from London!

Yours very gratefully,
Judith

From Judith Shakespeare to William Shakespeare

Dearest sir,

In answer to your last note to me, sir, with all respect let me say that you will deeply distress and mortify me to continue in your anxieties. Indeed, pursuant to your question, I know what I am about, and I assure you I have entered into no situation that will pose danger or harm to me, nor should distress you.

J. S.

From William Shakespeare to Judith Shakespeare

Daughter:

To hear of your engagement, rumors of which apparently run all over Stratford, not from you or your mother but from Bartholomew Hathaway! I am most mortified.

Your mother's brother, here on business, sought me out to tell me what all the village already knows. He was motivated by concern for you and what was due your family, and well he should be. I thank God he has alerted me to the goings-on.

I am not so harsh as to be completely unable to comprehend your own motivations for your behavior. You have, perhaps, never received the attention that was your due, from many quarters. But such a young man! And Margaret Wheeler close to her confinement—it is a matter universally talked of, according to your uncle; all the world knows the truth of it, no matter what the offender has told you.

I beseech you not to be hardened by the displeasure I have expressed, and to think of your own happiness and the man on whom all your future contentment will depend. Do not choose badly, my dear daughter. As clouds of my age gather in upon me, I begin more to think on you and Susanna. I would wish to see you well settled, Judith. Your mother and I will help you to some other solution, to something. Do not stay this course out of pride. It is not too late. Your happiness should not be sacrificed. Break if off now, however well known is the intention and your plans. We will weather the embarrassment together. I will support you in it.

Think on what I have said, daughter. It will take me perhaps a fortnight to arrange affairs with the theater so that I may leave for some weeks, but then I shall be at home, and we shall sort out all these matters. Do nothing in haste.

Does your hair continue so long and dark and rich, my dear? Your mother and I always did love to see it thus. I prefer dark hair, were you so aware? I came to be in the habit of praising fair hair, in verse, to please the queen when she was yet with us.

Adieu, your father,
William Shakespeare

From Judith Shakespeare to Susanna Hall

Susanna:

Master Adrian Quiney has come to see me. Apparently now there is a portion to be given to me to marry his grandson, rather than the other way around. His indiscretions, I am now told, require it.

One hundred pounds to my personal pocket, not jointly held but all mine, ready to be called upon after his death to support me in good fashion, better even than what father can bestow. All this to keep our engagement, to have him quickly married and settled and give at least the appearance of his having had nothing to do with poor Margaret Wheeler, now in the churchyard along with her child.

So. I am to be bribed to accept the hand of a man who made my heart flutter when first he offered it.

I should be astonished, I know, though the village is not. But I believed what he told me, when he told it. Yet somehow this latest turn seems quite expected. Perhaps the part of me that is so dark—do not deny it, sister, I know the town says so of me, "Judith Shakespeare, fine, upstanding, but a little—odd," they say. There are worse things to be, my dear sister—but I lose my thoughts, they are scattered, where were they? Yes, that part of me that is dark and odd. It knew. I did not listen to it much then. I confess 'twas a relief to be light and gay, made so by the attentions of a handsome man. He wanted me. I worried he would not come again on Saturdays, once he began. But he came, he did not leave off. And all thoughts were somehow made light by this.

Yet my darkness knew.

I sat up all last night, though I burned perhaps a dozen candles. Mother, I am sure, had not the heart to disturb me, though she knew not the particular cause of my distress, only I am sure surmised it to have to do with Thomas. I suppose it is thanks be to God that due to Father we need not conserve candles, even now, in this late, endless, wet winter. There were no books in my room, and for some reason I wished not to venture into the hall—wished not to meet Mother or any of the servants, even in passing. And so I contented myself with, of all tomes, our father's manuscript, yet to be sent off to him in London—forgive me for forgetting, dear sister, I know you asked it be done, but you must own my mind has been much occupied of late. I had laid it in all absence of thought upon my dressing table when young Percy brought it to me, the better to hunt for a coin and read your note, and then did forget it. And perhaps I do not carry out our father's requests for little tasks as quickly as an obedient daughter might.

In any case, I picked it up—perhaps I wished to find some weakness in it, and point it out to you or myself, for some strange satisfaction. However, I find it is beautifully writ. As always with Father, especially now, so late in his life, no flaw can be found in his verse, no twist of plot unfitting or turn of human nature unaccounted for in his plays.

I shall tell you the story, Susanna, and you will be interested. A great old king sadly mistreats his daughter, abandoning her to her fate, which plunges him into great catastrophes, each building upon the other. She keeps to her integrity and virtue, loving him ever, and when he finally sees her again after his great miseries, knowing all his wrongs and brought low and half mad, he asks her forgiveness, though he knows she has cause to withhold it. She replies, "No cause, no cause." I was quite astonished at how my own emotion was moved by the scene—but again, there is no denying the skill of the pen that rendered it.

Is it not strange that our father should write such a thing? I never knew he thought much on the heart or mind of a daughter, did you? Do you suppose he wishes all daughters held in their bosoms such mercy? That fathers should be received so?

Wondrous thing it would be, if they did. And if a father, at such a late hour in life, did tender his affection to a daughter left alone.

My dear sister, I do not write you for advice on my course with Thomas. Only because it is early morn now, the last candle sputters, and I wish to unburden my heart. I think I must accept the offer of the Quineys, Susanna. Else what would become of me?

Do not tell mother or father of this arrangement between me and Thomas's grandfather Adrian, I beg you. I truly wish that no one ever know.

It is possible that the next time I have occasion to write you a note, instead of walking across the village to your house, I shall be Mrs. Quiney.

Your beloved sister,

Judith Shakespeare

From Judith Shakespeare to William Shakespeare

My very dear father,

Herewith I send you the play that you did leave

with my sister when last you were home, hoping it shall find you before you leave London, as you said you were about to do and which now surely you must, so to attend my wedding.

Come, Father, shall we be perfect friends again?

For the last time I sign,

Judith Shakespeare

From William Shakespeare to Judith Shakespeare

My dear Judith:

Adrian Quiney has writ to me. What am I to say? Nothing, so I understand. Your mother tells me you ask that this arrangement between you and the esteemed grandsire of Thomas Quiney never be spoken of, that no record of it ever be struck. Very well, then. I shall never speak of it. But you cannot deny me, daughter, to write of it.

I reminded your mother of our late queen, who did choose to live alone and by the grace of God to so well govern her subjects, and she reminds me that the queen may have done as she pleased, but that the world of Stratford is a different place from that which surrounded Her Majesty.

Yet I feel I have mayhap led you to this place, Judith, or left you alone in it, I know not which. I have provided for you in a material way but in some other way not, and somehow that is the cause that you find yourself (I shall be blunt, you appreciate plain speech) thirty and an old maid with no hope of companionship when your mother and I are gone, save this path that lies before you.

And now Margaret Wheeler is dead in the church-yard, alone but for her babe. I would not have you skirt close to the same fate—and I am told that somehow this other fate you are being paid to take is preferable. And so I consent, my dear, if it is truly the course you wish.

And I ask you, my daughter, to forgive me.

What will you answer, my dear? Will you yet tell me that there is no cause necessitates forgiveness? Or will you, all your days, wish that I could have made this right for you, got you a proper man, a good husband, and a life gone some other road?

The horses are brought. I will see you e'er you see this.

Your loving father,
William Shakespeare

The Scottish Wife

In honor of my husband's victory at Peter's Heath, the king has called for great revels to greet the new year at Lady Day. Of course, it is only I call it my husband's victory. All others call it Duncan's, the king's, though it was my own lord, Macbeth, who strategized in the field, led the foot soldiers to their deaths for Duncan's glory with warm and encouraging words, and killed more Cornishmen than Scottish when he was through. The king was warm at camp on high ground, fallen back five miles. To ensure that his officers would not lose him. Or his leadership abilities.

His feast tonight is certainly one of victory, such as would be hosted by a gracious and benevolent leader. We sit on the fancy crafted benches, not merely trestles, at the tables covered with meats, some ground to a paste with bits of fruit, some roasted, whole boars, flavorings of garlic and onions and wine. Ale and more wine are ever flowing and silver knives lie at every place. My lord feeds me, as all the lords do their ladies, giving me bits of delicacies from his knife that I reach for with my tongue and swallow, washing them down my throat with more red wine.

When we have all eaten Duncan calls his advisers and great officers to council. My lord is talking to the elegant

Lady Macduff—I have encouraged it, her husband is an important man, and my own lord may be made less uneasy by a woman than by a thane of great influence. But my heart sinks when I see him. I am looking about for him to prompt him to hear the king and gather with his fellows. He is shifting uneasily from one foot to the other, unaware of it, and laughing loudly at his own jokes. The lady endures it, smiling politely, but I can see from across the length of the great hall that she wishes him gone. I make my way to them.

"Husband, I believe the king has called for you," I say, and she gives me a look of gratitude for the rescue. I do not look back at her. I will take no part in any look that doubts my husband's worth. When we reach Duncan, he is surrounded by the thane of Cawdor; Macduff, the thane of Fife; Ross, Lennox, Menteith, and Macdonwald; my husband's gentle friend Banquo and even Banquo's oldest boy.

"We will retire and hear what our trusty and most beloved friend Ross has to tell us on the subject of his expedition to Ireland," Duncan intones. "And we will discuss, if called for, the preliminary measures for an effort into the area."

"Indeed, sir," Ross begins, too eager even to wait until they are all sitting in the privy council's chamber, "I do believe the place could be a rich source of slaves, our suppositions are borne out, and could bring a great deal of wealth to the nation—" He stops. The king is no longer looking at him, but has seen my lord.

"Ah, Macbeth!" He is, for a moment, perplexed. Then, "I think we may do without you here. We have voices enough for tonight."

All are silent. All know what the king has just done to my lord.

I say, "The king is concerned that you rest at home and deal with your daily affairs, settle with the steward, my love, as befits a gentleman of property, before entering into another service for him. You have been gone from home so long. You have not slept in your own bed a night. We thank you for the honor, Your Grace."

"Yes, yes, well said, lady," says the king, his tartan flung casually over his shoulder, his magnificent head thickly covered with snowy hair. How easily he wears his power. Almost. He is at this moment thinking about looking as though he wears his power easily. But it is not effortless, it is not assured. Because I am a woman and notice the degree of comfort of others, I can see this where the great lords cannot.

I want to cry at them, "Does my husband not already feel *enough* alone? Must you find yet one more enterprise from which to shut him out? What harm, what harm in letting him sit with you, make a suggestion? You would only bury any words of his in any case. Why can you not even allow him into the council chamber?" I want to scream, "He is in your service every day, Your Grace, seldom at home, sleeping on the ground, going forward in damp wool and chain mail onto wet sodden fields for *you*, like a dog, with vain hopes you will show him the courtesy you show your hounds, and pat his head. Yet you do not. Can you not see how wounded he is? How can you not? I can!"

And in my mind I see, as I have so often seen before, myself tearing their eyes out, flaying them all, their groans of agony as I stack their skins on the ground beside them. Why, why, why heap so many humiliations upon my husband?

There is nothing so very wrong with him. His face is not so very comely, but it is open and pleasant. He has a broad brow, with wide-set large eyes and wide thick eyebrows; the largeness of his eyes gives him an innocent manner, a look always like that of a child. Is this one of the reasons the king does not hear my lord with the gravity with which he would hear Macduff, or that skinny, wormlike creature with the little sharp nose and mouth, the thane of Cawdor? When my lord smiles, which is not often, and even less often now than it once was—he smiled on our wedding night, at me—his mouth is broad, and has an element of flashing light in it. And my lord is not tall, but his chest and shoulders are very round and strong, like great barrels. I try to smooth his path.

He is a talented field general; why does no one see it? He won the battle of Peter's Heath using the longbow, his forces two thousand against the Cornish ten. Of course, the Cornish archers had only crossbows, and their knights would not fight on foot, they felt it was beneath them; they clung on their horses and lost, the fools. But two thousand against ten thousand! Surely my lord deserved more than the "Well done, loyal servant" that the king dished up.

Now, at home, I seethe in the warmly lit antechamber outside our bedroom, next to the hissing fire. When my husband comes in from seeing the porter and making sure all is secure for the night, he says, his voice dead, "I am accustomed to it, as you know, my love. Do not be so angry."

"I feel for you! Can you not feel for yourself?"

"Perhaps."

I reach for him, to shake his shoulders, but he catches my arms. An odd action, I know, for a little thing like me to shake a man so big as him, yet we have got in the habit of it.

He says, "But this does not assist me, this vengefulness of yours. It only makes me believe myself even less worthy a man. You will cease."

"Yes, my lord." He is my husband, my lord, my master, after all. Yet only some seconds later my voice is raised again, in a way I cannot desist or hold within. "I would they were dead, all of them. No, that would not hurt them enough. I would their children were dead."

Now he lets go my arms. I think he does not wish to touch me when I am this way. "That is horrible," he says. "Beg pardon of God."

"God is on our side and will favor us, if he does not now."

He looks at me, into my eyes. "You were not so when we were married. I do not feel these things so. How is it that you feel them more than I?"

He has no idea, then, what it has been to watch him these more than dozen years. And he lies, though he may yet know it not. He feels these things no less than I. Else why would he say what he says in other moods, talk of losing the many races he is losing with the other officers, with that snake Cawdor? I know how my lord Macbeth watches the thane of Cawdor and quietly figures the youth of that arrogant man.

"Let's to bed," I say. It has been a difficult night, this night. All will be well in the morning. He will forget my bitter words that show me to be horrible. He knows how I love him.

* * *

My marriage bed is covered with the skins of gray wolves, a present from him to me on our wedding day to show his bravery. That day was the first I ever saw of my husband, dark-eyed young Macbeth. Tonight he sleeps before I do.

My husband provides for us well; we have never wanted for a stable stronghold, never suffered from debt. I have given him sons to his liking, a home always warm and welcoming and well ordered, a happy bed. I have always provided for his comfort. He has rewarded me with kindness—even now he is far kinder to me than ever my father was—and gratitude. He is grateful to me for my face and my love, for being beautiful. I once was able to talk my lord into more cheerful moods when he was kicking at himself, but less so now, though he kicks with more and more ferocity. And so I give it up, and am more and more ferocious myself. I am out of patience.

My love stirs in his sleep as I turn beneath the skins of the wolves. His sleep is delicate. He is easily chilled, or fevered, or beset by nightmares. Of late he is plagued by weird women who speak to him in his dreams of bloody battles and cold heaths. "My poor dear," I say now as he breathes quickly and wakes with a tiny cry. He tried to cry out in his dream, no doubt, and could not. "Is your sleep disturbed again? You must forget such childish nonsense. Let me bathe your temples for you."

And I put my little bare foot out of the bed despite the cold of the stony floor, to go out of the room again for the cloth and basin of water in the antechamber.

"No," he says. "No. Stay."

I have not yet put out my candle and in its light I see there is more silver shining in my husband's hair than I have yet noticed. I stroke the silver.

"Are you counting how many white hairs I have?" he snaps. He does not intend the sharpness of his voice. I know this.

"No, sweetheart," I answer. "The shadows are of my candle, love, not your age."

He smiles a small, stingy smile, not the smile I have known.

"Forgive me," he says. "Now that you are here I will sleep again. I will sleep sound."

He does fall asleep again in moments, beneath the gray skins of the wolves, and in his sleep he reaches for me and puts his head on my breast, as he has every night we have passed together since we married.

I will have no more of his unhappiness. I will no more watch him suffer. This must all end.

Sitting up beneath these animals on this bed, my head against an everyday bolster of scratchy wool, I look at the stones of the wall, smell the smoke of the dying bedroom fire. The lines between the stones seem to move in the deceitful candlelight, and I think I see a way.

It may not yet be too late for him. He shall have what he desires. I will it, and I shall do it, with or without his help. I will speak of it to him tomorrow.

"Sweetest love," I whisper in his sleeping ear.

My parents married me to him when I was twelve and he twenty-two, and I was happy. He was not ugly, and he was steady. Other girls might marry old men, or hard men who beat them. Not I.

"Are you happy it was me, lady?" he would sometimes suddenly ask, after we had been quiet for a time, sitting together. He still does sometimes.

"Yes, my lord." I would smile and curl up against him. Oh, I was a little bit of a thing at twelve, and he already big and burly. The fathers of some of the other ladies shunned young Macbeth; they saw how he was too aware of himself, always ill at ease, and they feared he would not do well enough to make the alliance of value, despite his talent in the field. But my father was the youngest son of a youngest son, and bitter at his lot, with almost no portion to give with me, and so to Macbeth I was given myself. And I warmed to my new husband. He liked to please me with gifts and baubles, pearls and silks and trinkets and ornaments, as though I were a little girl. My father had only sharp words for me and slaps when I questioned him, but my lord asked my advice on gestures of tribute for the king, thanked me when the king expressed appreciation.

But that was years ago now.

This morning, after my night awake beneath the wolves, watching the stones of our walls, my husband says to me, "I am not twenty-five anymore. I am not even thirty-five anymore."

We are sitting by another fire, not the large one in the great hall or antechamber but a small one we have caused to be lit in our private dining parlor, after breakfast, against the gloomy sky and dark of the rooms. The steward awaits him in the hall. After so long an absence from home as my husband had on the last campaign, there is much business to settle, accounts to reconcile, that I as a woman may not put my hand to. I have asked if he would like me to go over the correspondence of the last weeks with him, but he did not wish it. So we stare into the fire. Dully, he rises to go to attend to the steward.

"Wait, husband," I say. "I wish to consult you."

He smiles but without happiness. "Aye, lady?" he says. "Advice from me? And not Cawdor? He received another honor from the king this morning, did you not hear? The messenger came before you were up, and he summons me to court tomorrow, and told me of this. Perhaps Cawdor may offer better counsel."

"My lord, this is unworthy! Again I must beg you not to compare yourself with the thane of Cawdor. I must enumerate again the many advantages he has had that my lord has not—his father's land holdings were second only to the king's; his birth, through no fault of any but God, sir, is higher than yours. The king feared old Cawdor's soldiers; he fears also young Cawdor's soldiers! So he favored the old man while he lived and favors his son now for his own safety's sake. You know this, my lord. That is why Cawdor began his career so early, and under the king's special protection. It was no merit of his. You are just as good a soldier, perhaps better. I have told you all this before."

And I rise without knowing it, and reach to shake his shoulders again, with anger, like a mother after a child who has run in front of a cart, who cries as she shakes, "Never, never do such a thing again!"

Outside the stone and earthen walls of our keep a wolf howls—odd, in the morning. Yet the sky is so greenish gray and hellish outside that perhaps the poor dumb beast is confused.

"Cawdor is ahead of me," he says. "It does not signify why. I am far behind. I do not know if I can ever catch up. Cawdor has been made the lord protector of the Western Isles; he commands an entire company now in the name of Duncan the king. He is exempted from a part of the farming revenues due the crown. His rise is unstoppable."

"Almost."

Cawdor is greedy. I know.

When we married my lord talked to me expansively of favors he would win, advances he would make, a stroke of luck to come to him that would turn to an opportunity well taken. But such things never came. He no longer speaks to me of his dreams.

"I never understood why you did not take on the voyage to Ireland, as Ross did, to investigate the possibility of the Irish slave trade . . . ," I begin.

"Because it would take too long," he answers, still standing by the fire. "By the time I returned, Ross might have advanced himself further, and then I would not have fared any better in comparison to the other lords than when I left Scotland! And perhaps I might have failed entirely, and be a great deal worse off, and then the household would be in debt and the children would have no inheritance, and then I would have even less influence at court, after all the costs of outfitting the expedition. . . ." The words spiral down and down. In these moments he feels himself less worthy than he did even before he began his speech. *Why?* I ask the heavens. Why should he be so tormented?

But he can yet win his race if he runs ever more quickly now.

"So," he says, and sits down by me again shamefaced, on the tapestry footrest, not the wooden chair covered with rich cushions of my own working. "I am most humbly sorry, lady. You support me in my efforts. You encouraged me, I do remember, about Ireland. I am grateful."

"I am often too hot as well, husband. I beg your forgiveness. I will try to temper myself."

His reaches out his large hand to encircle my ankle, absently stroking it, as he often quietly did when we first married and I lay beside him beneath the animal skins.

"On what shall you seek my advice, my dear?" he asks.

My lips are dry, perhaps from the smoky air of the fire. I lick them. "I think, my love, that Cawdor is about something."

Silence. My husband does not move. His next speech is slow, and suddenly quiet. Yet he does not put any emphasis on the word, as though he is merely curious.

"Why?"

And now I am excited, and I speak quickly, however careful his talk may be.

"I saw him at the feast for Lady Day. He was looking—only looking, mind, not even smiling—at Macdonwald. The look was overlong. No other lady saw, I am sure, they were all conversing about nothing. I happened to raise my eyes to the thane. They looked at each other overlong, husband. They are in league. They are plotting."

He is not looking at me but into the fire, his gray eyes unblinking. I go on.

"Cawdor wants his benefactor's throne, my love. If he is found out, then his fate is sealed, and he can pain you no more—the fact of him shall be removed. But what's more, and of much more importance, is that there is opportunity for you, for us. We must act quickly, have all our plans ready."

I pause—perhaps he will want to say something? No. Well, then.

"With Cawdor out of the way, his own heirs disinherited, as they must be under the penalty for treason, his lands confiscated, given to another"—and here my voice is slow and deliberate for the space of a few words—"perhaps even to you, you would be in a position to try for the throne upon the king's death."

"The king has sons," my love says quietly, his voice going up in tone at the end of his sentence as though he asks a question.

"That can be—arranged."

"I see."

I wait now.

"You plan, then, lady, to unmask Cawdor to the king?"

"Oh no, no."

"No? How else to win the king's favor? How else to bring all of this about?"

"Listen to me. Truly listen. We will allow the thane of Cawdor to undertake his rebellion. You, you will be prepared, you will battle him, reach the field first, and kill all who support him there. Together, then, when the thane is dead and the king is in your debt, we will begin our work. We will"—and I whisper—"deal, my lord, with the king, afterward. If he is not killed in the rebellion, well. We will deal with him."

And still he stares into the fire, and I wait and wait, and for the sake of Christ, will he only say a word, one word? The fire crackles and pops. The new wood hisses there in the grate.

And when I have given up hope of his words, he speaks.

"I cannot do such a thing. You talk treason."

"By heaven!" I whisper. "Enough! How long have I known you, my lord? How well? How long loved you? I have dispelled your downcast moods, I have propped you up in that pit of snakes at court, I have helped you in every way, and you must own that."

"I do, I—"

"There is always a reason you cannot!" I make my voice more tender. "I can hear, I swear to you, the ceaseless voices that chime in your poor head, that keep you hobbled with your 'I cannot' and your 'but what if.'"

"Valiance and hard work—"

"Will bring you nothing."

"Yes, you have said so before, why talk of this now?"

"Because I will stand by and watch such things no more. You cannot do this thing? Well, then, you need not. I will determine all. Beginning this morning, I will be the field general. I want only the best for you. Only to see you happy. Do you know this?"

He looks up. He knows. He knows the thing will happen. It has been set in motion, even now. It will not be stopped. I have seen the cracks in the wall and I know where they go, and what follows them.

It may not be enough. Men like my husband can never find glory enough for themselves in the eyes of the world, because there is none in their own eyes. And he may come to hate me for what we are about to do, for how I ensure that we hammer away at the cracks in the wall between him and his ambition, for how the cracks will grow and spread and shatter what was. It will remind him that he feels he is weak. And perhaps I will hate him for it, because I had to take matters, finally, into my woman's hands.

But this morning, I love him. He wants something so much, so deservedly. It is simple, what he wants. And all I want is to give it to him, even over his objections if so it must be.

"Listen, my dear love," I begin. "When you are victorious . . . the king will pay us the honor of a visit . . . you see? In our home . . . alone, only a token entourage, he will be almost unguarded . . . you understand? It is a simple plan . . . listen . . ."

"In our *home*?" He pulls away, stares at me. "My king? You would have me be Judas?"

I meet his eye. I am not afraid. I love him.

"I would. And betray his sons, too, all his pretty ones. For you. Only for you."

It is tenderness that drives me. Oh, my husband, my poor little boy, with his head in my lap. I lean down to him on the footrest, to kiss him. His mouth opens beneath mine and he grips me. He holds my shoulders hard, digging in the tips of his fingers. We are breathless.

By hell, I will kill the king, if he cannot.

The fire crackles, and my dear love speaks.

"As you wish, lady."

Diamonds at Her Fingertips

The master was dying. He knew everyone knew it, everyone said it, even when they were around him. They whispered it when they thought he could not hear. They exchanged looks as they moved his great, shiplike bed with him in it to the kitchen on the ground floor of his big beautiful house—New Place, in Stratford, the house that he had so often passed on the way to school and longed to live in as a child. The great kitchen was comfortably warm and red, and he was happy there.

He was dying. Beneath his terror, at another, deeper plane, he felt oddly relaxed about the whole business.

He knew his good fortune. He had spent his time on earth in doing what called to him and doing it extremely well, to accolades that did not take so very long in coming. Not a wasted life—no, not wasted at all. His illness was an unspecified fever, possibly influenza or pneumonia. A normal illness, not too unbearably painful in its ravages, its harvesting of body and soul. The master was an intelligent, creative man, and as pleased their majesties, a Protestant rather than a Catholic. As such he had always been skeptical of horrors that might be awaiting him for unexpurgated sins, despite the warnings he had put into the mouth of the ghostly father of his tortured Danish hero, his saddest, most beloved son, Hamlet, and despite that he knew himself no saint.

He did regret that he had not known the queen when she was young.

When he himself was middle-aged, well established entertaining her in her private theater, and she old and painted, he heard her say from his place on the stage as Duke Theseus, "I am married to England," to one of her ministers. He turned his eyes toward her and saw her show the old counselor her ruby coronation ring, now sized for her wedding finger. Painted or not, she was dazzling, all in white, her gown embroidered with pearls, hundreds of them, set in place with knots of silver thread. When enough pearls could not be found for the gown she used twopenny beads from the market to fill it—the costume masters for the Earl's Men heard of that, as they could not get a false pearl for weeks on account of it. Real or false, the effect was the important thing; she understood that, as did he and other men of the theater. For the event held to honor the Dutch ambassador, the ballroom in the palace was splendid, hung with cloth of silver and white, fiery with the light of a thousand candles in candelabras, but she shone and glittered in it. There had been songs and dancing celebrating English pirates, followed by his own play, full of gamboling fairies and Robin Goodfellow and the pagan woods of his childhood and weddings, many weddings, double, triple, quadruple marriages at the finish.

She was fond of saying she was married to England. As though that were the same as being married to a person. Well, it was not.

It is my birthday, he suddenly thought. It was. It is my

birthday and I think I am about to die. His wife, Anne, sitting on a plain wooden stool beside the huge bed by the fire, seemed to hear; she leaned in toward him. Her hair, gray now, was carefully coifed in a manner completely appropriate to her age and her position as the wife of a country gentleman: no flounces or elaborate curls too young for her, but a row of simple, elegant chignons across the back of her neck beneath her cap. She had always known how to look lovely, just right. When he was only eighteen he had been at the mercy of her warm, round body and her red hair.

"Day," he said, trying to voice his thoughts. But however lucid his mind, he could not make his mouth follow suit. He wanted to talk about his birthday and his death, but he could manage no more than, again, "Day."

"Yes, husband, it is day now," Anne answered.

He shook his head petulantly, like a child. He gathered his strength. "No," he forced out, then wanted only to sleep. Such a fate, he thought, for a man like me. I can no longer send my words from my mouth or my fingers to the eyes and ears of others. He began to weep, silently, and he felt the warm drops slide from the corners of his eyes down his temples. Even as he noticed the dampness on the pillow he reflected that his sheets were dry and cool despite his fever and sweating, and he knew that Anne and his daughters must be taking great care to keep him comfortable. The sheets were not the rough everyday ones, but the smooth linen, for company, usually kept on the great carved guest bed that he and Anne never slept in.

His wife called to someone unseen, just beyond the

kitchen door. A servant, or perhaps one of his daughters. Her voice was tight with urgency. "Send for John!"

He knew she meant John Hall, his daughter Susanna's husband. John was a physician; it was he who had recommended his removal to the kitchen, for the warmth and so that the patient could be more easily attended to. Anne's voice, however tense, had calmed the master. He wanted to tell her not to worry. His mood had swung completely in a second, like a clock pendulum, and he was suddenly floating, rising above his sadness at his loss of his words. He needed no new words, surely? His old words, words already set down, were there, he thought, resigned and philosophic. They would be there for a bit more time, at least.

"He was the greatest writer ever born." He opened his eyes. John Hall was there—when had he come? Was it he who had said those words? He did not think so. John was not a great reader. He must have dreamt them. The greatest writer ever born? He knew there was no such thing. He might have been a genius—he did think that was possible. He was never sure. He was prolific, he would give himself that, scratching away in London, first in a room above a dairy with nothing but a heap of straw on a bed frame, then in progressively more luxurious lodgings. But to write a great deal was not genius, it was only picking up the pen without caring if he were inspired or not. There really were not so many stories in the world.

The housekeeper came in; he could hear her gait, uneven but sure, as she carried the cordials and cool cloths that she handed to Anne. John was gone, and the light that flowed through the kitchen door seemed different, more blue than gold. He thought he saw shadows cast by the fire on the brick-red stones of the floor. Perhaps he had slept and it was evening.

"And how is the master, mistress?"

"More poorly, I am afraid, Mary," said his wife.

He smiled, although he did not know if the smile arrived at his lips. He liked old Mary Quickly.

The servant peered at his face. He tried to focus his eyes to look back at her, but he could not.

"By my maidenhead at twelve years old, mistress, he does look ill," she said. "Well, if he doth recover, 'tis the will of God and the Virgin; and if he doth not, 'tis the same."

"I should not like him upset, Mary—"

"Ach! If he hears me, he knows 'tis true." She spoke very close to his face, and he saw the spiderweb of lines. "Is it not true, master? Death is but a little thing; you are not afraid of it, are you? There is no need. Only a blink, and then you find yourself in the greenwoods of your child's days, surrounded by young virgins! Ah, that will bring you back to life!"

He saw Anne smile in spite of herself. Anne, who sprang from the greenwoods of his memories. He loved Anne. He loved women. Many-faceted jewels, he thought, so strong. Essential to a plot. And so tender at night. He had never done well without them.

Now his wife, no doubt tired, called his younger daughter to stay with him awhile. "Judith! Judith, come in now, stay by your father. I must attend to some things." He heard Judith's step, heavy though she was a thin thing. Judith—his dead son, Hamnet's, twin—sat by his side to stay with him awhile. His little boy, long gone; yes, that he regretted.

"How are you, Father?" she asked, taking her place as her mother stood.

"I do not think he can answer you, daughter."

He would try. "I regret," he wanted to say, and his lips moved. He did not think he had said it. Perhaps he need not try to say "I." Perhaps that would be understood. He tried again. "Regret."

Judith bent her ear to his mouth. Her dark, thin hair brushed his cheek, and the softness of it was soothing, like a feather on his skin. He wished she would stay that way awhile. He had no way to tell her this. Again he tried: "Regret."

He did not think she understood, but she sat upright again and patted his arm. "It is all right, Father," she said. "Everything is all right." He hoped she meant that all in his life was forgiven. He hoped she was not merely humoring him. It was hard to tell with Judith.

Today Judith simply sat on the stool by the side of his bed. She did not read or sew. The few times he opened his eyes, he saw that she looked at him. She was not so very young now, either, and her skin, so fair, showed new fine lines around her eyes and mouth.

He wished for his boy. But he knew he did not regret as he should have the abandonment of his family. Rightly or wrongly, he believed for many years that it had done no real harm to leave his wife in the country alone while he pursued his calling in London, or to never know his children very well. Like many men, he sorted things into separate boxes in his mind and heart: home, here; work, there; love, there. And like many men he convinced himself that he was not really wanted in places where he did not wish to be. He was providing for his family, after all; they would never have to worry after his death. They had had resources at home in Stratford. His children never wanted for love or attention from relatives, and his wife had no wish to be part of the world of the theater.

His constant companion in London was fear, but not in the way in which it is usually understood. Fear had been there when he wrote his poor Hamlet's speech of apology to Laertes, whose father the prince of Denmark had killed, sending Laertes into a misery parallel to his own. Hamlet, like Laertes, had been about to die, and had great foreboding. But it was a sweet speech, generous and full of love and humility, not courtly obligation. The master had been—still was—proud of it, though it was not so musical as some of his others, not so widely quoted.

He found it did not work to bury the fear or push it aside. He was quite used to it after thirty years. Fear was his partner. He might have felt odd without it; or he might not. It fought with him, when his work began to open a way to show himself to the world; to show himself angry, or arrogant, or tender. But he wrestled it, every time; despite its rigid grip on his heart and thoughts it had wings, and he coaxed it to the ceiling, to the roof, to fly away, again and again.

The queen had helped him. She ensured him money, fame, standing. She understood his sons and daughters walking the stage, the fearful ones, the proud ones, the unhappy ones. How sweet the queen must once have been. How clever. And she must have known real fear, a fear so old it became a bedfellow, like his. She scratched with a diamond on the window of the room where her sister, Queen Mary, kept her in the Tower, still a teenager:

Much suspected of me
Nothing proved can be
Elizabeth, prisoner.

The master loved that! It reminded him of his own pithy asides, quick and rhyming, humor glistening through grimness, the dark, dark humor he so enjoyed. Written with a diamond by an imprisoned princess! Imprisoned by her own sister, and always suspected a bastard, until the growing wealth of England under her guidance, and her own will, changed people's minds. Her mother so publicly murdered, years before. Scratched with a diamond. He could not have invented better.

She was like his dear boy Hamlet. Her mother's murderer was her father, the king, and she was dependent on his favor for her life. But in another way she was not like his prince; she had no sword or rights of injured manhood. Poor child. She must have been very different the day she became queen from the woman, fifty-nine years old, who welcomed him at court, he only in his twenties, in awe. The woman who said to him, as he knelt before her after a performance of *As You Like It*, in a ballroom unspeakably luxurious, paneled in gold and jewels, "Stand up straight, boy, and say something with that silver tongue that I have so enabled! And eating cakes of leavening may help to arrest that unfortunate direction of the line of your hair."

Judith stirred. "Yes, Father, I have changed my hair. Mother, come quickly, I believe he is more himself!"

Her Majesty must have been beautiful when she became queen, a bit odd, yes, with a face too narrow, a nose too long and thin, with a fine hook. Eyes too close together, like his. Almost too pale. How many of his heroines he had made pale to flatter her. So vain, his queen, so vain, that *woman* . . .

"Woman? Yes, husband, I am here."

He focused his eyes with great effort. It was his wife, Anne, there now. Anne. Good.

He knew the cause of the queen's vanity. She felt herself poorly formed, like his Richard of York, but from within, not without, and she never got the better of it. No matter how adored she was, no matter that she was queen. Her mother murdered, her father an imposing, capricious giant, even her young stepmother dragged away and beheaded. The little princess alternately called for and sent away, the king haunted by his sins in her innocent face, she always thinking there was some correct answer for him, but there never was. Who could wonder that Elizabeth would never marry? A pack of clod-minded politicians, that was who. The poets and players all understood quick enough.

He would have liked to have written her story but he could not. No one dared; it went unspoken. And she still seemed to love her father's memory; she mentioned him reverently in her speeches. He knew he could not have loved such a father. Women were different.

She must have been beautiful. But that was not the reason he wished he had known her when she was young. Nor was it her power. She had done enough for him, more than enough. Her favor had made him rich. He only thought that when she was young, the queen might have liked to sit and talk to him. He thought that might have eased her mind.

He might have helped her, if he had known her when she was young. Despite his cleverness and his skill with words—what a refuge the English language had been to him!—he listened well. He heard now the sound of his own breath, startling the woman at his bedside. It was not Anne. It was old Mary. Yes, I'm still here, he thought, but not for long. Dear God, this is lonesome. Did my little boy feel so alone? He was terribly thirsty.

"I think of rain," he said, and Mary caught her breath. He realized he had uttered all four words aloud. He did not know how. Perhaps because he had not been trying. Sometimes the words come when one is not trying.

Mary was skilled enough to know that if the master was thinking of water he was likely to want to drink, and put a cup to his lips. "There, there, sir, it won't be long until rain," she said. "It is a showery April." Liar, he thought. Even he could tell that outside the sun shone.

He was quiet again. The queen appeared before him, effervescent, waiting. "Lady!" he called, and Anne hurried to him. So he had made his voice heard once more. But it was not Anne he called.

He saw the queen once before he came to London. When he was eleven she came to Kenilworth Castle, near Stratford, for three weeks of festivities planned for her by the earl of Leicester. There were fireworks, and a new pond dug in the shape of a crescent moon, symbol of Diana, to honor her—and plays. His father hired him out to help the earl's troupe about the stage, to bring in some money. They were in need of it; his father was in terrible debt. He saw her only once, only the ruff of her stiff collar, spangled with gold stars. He thought her fingers must be tipped with diamonds instead of fingernails. He stood behind a door stage left, holding swords for the players. He could never see her face, she had so very many lords around her. But the gold stars glowed with the magic of her, and he knew he would follow her, like a goddess, to beyond the ends of the earth.

Author's Note

Shakespeare scholars will notice that I have sometimes compressed the time line of the Bard's life, particularly toward the end of his years. William Shakespeare is generally, although not universally, assumed to have retired to Stratford by the time he was deposed regarding Mary Mountjoy, and before his daughter Judith had married. Adrian Quiney, grandfather of Judith's husband, Thomas Quiney, was already dead by then, and Richard Quiney, Thomas's father, had, in fact, been murdered. The record shows that Shakespeare paid for his house, New Place, a few months after his son died, so it is likely that the boy actually died at Shakespeare's father's house; because the only information we have about this child is the dates of his baptism and burial, we will probably never even know the cause of his death.

It may be of interest to readers to note that the poems on pages 56 and 167 are attributed to Queen Elizabeth I.

I wish particularly to acknowledge my debt to Park Honan's *Shakespeare: A Life,* from Oxford University Press, a new and definitive biography that separates fact from legend and explores more fully than its predecessors the likely circumstances of Shakespeare's relationships with the women of his family and work; and also to the New Folger Library Editions of Shakespeare's plays.

Acknowledgments

I am very happy and proud to be able to thank the many people I have had the incredible good fortune to have as teachers, friends, and well-wishers, and who helped and encouraged me to make this project a reality. To my advisers at Warren Wilson College's master of fine arts program, Robert Boswell, C. J. Hribal, Joan Silber, and Chuck Wachtel; as well as to many other teachers at the program, Andrea Barrett, Charles Baxter, Karen Brennan, Kevin McIlvoy, Rick Russo, Peter Turchi, and Geoffrey Wolff; and to all the other talented, generous, and kind people there, I owe a great debt. They are very special, and I thank them for teaching me how to begin to learn to write. I owe a similar debt to my first writing teacher, Thaisa Frank, who gave me the freedom to explore. And thank you to Robin Maxwell, who was never too busy to encourage and advise a fledgling writer.

My gratitude to my agent, Jenny Bent, is beyond expression; her upbeat energy and enthusiasm infect all who meet her, and her support for this book has changed my life. What would I do without her? Gratitude is also due to my outstanding editor, Kris Puopolo, for her warmth, her intelligence, her frank feedback, and her crucial support.

To my dear friend and teacher in writing and all things, Philip Herter, thank you. Thank you to Marcella Friel,

Acknowledgments

Dorothy Hearst, and Carolyn Uno, unflagging supporters of my writing and my dreams, the three great goddesses who reminded me again and again that I could do it. Thank you to those rare, true friends who have unfailingly been there for me, the ones I always know I can call in the middle of a dark night: Neil Bason, Tom Bemis, Cathy Bowman, Susan Eigenbrodt, Leslie Katz, Pam MacLean, Tom Murphy, Erika Nanes, Lisa Olsen, Alice Rowan, Laurel Scheinman, and my beloved sister, Brenna Hopkins. More thanks to my dear friends and colleagues in the land of publishing: Elizabeth Forsaith, Judith Hibbard, Lorri Wimer, and Jeff Wyneken. Thank you to my parents, Marv and Barbara, who made me a writer.

Finally, I want to say thank you with love to my husband, Mehran Saky. I often wonder what I did to deserve to be so lucky as to have found him waiting for me.

About the Author

PAMELA RAFAEL BERKMAN was born in Chicago. She has worked as a reporter, freelance writer, and editor for San Francisco Bay area newspapers, magazines, wire services, and Jossey-Bass publishing. Her articles and reviews have appeared in the *San Francisco Examiner,* the *San Francisco Bay Guardian,* and the *Oakland Tribune.* Her 1998 short story "The Falling Nun" was nominated for a Pushcart Prize. She currently works as an editor and lives in Berkeley with her husband, filmmaker Mehran Saky.

DISCUSSION POINTS

1. What is your opinion of historical fiction? Can it enhance your understanding of historical fact? Do you need to be familiar with Shakespeare's plays or his biography to enjoy this book? Discuss how one of Berkman's stories stands alone.

2. How do these stories reveal the quality of everyday life for Shakespeare's mother, his wife, his London landlady, and even Queen Elizabeth? How do these stories influence your thinking about the roles of the women in his life, and the women of his times? How does Shakespeare come across during his interactions with, and his thoughts about, women?

3. Explore how the story "In the Bed" traces the evolution of Will and Anne's love and marriage. What do the different bedroom scenes reveal about the changes in their relationship?

4. Titania is afraid that without William Shakespeare she "will surely die." Why? What is happening to her world of ancient beliefs and ritual? Why does she wholeheartedly approve of Anne Shakespeare?

5. "Jennet" portrays *Hamlet* as arising out of a particular moment in Shakespeare's life. How do Will and Jennet's shared experiences of loss advance Will's development of his Hamlet character? Describe Will and Jennet's relationship.

6. In "Dark Blue," what is Ophelia's reaction to her first stirrings of sexual attraction toward Hamlet? How do her feelings about her sexuality differ from her father and brother's attitude? How does Berkman express Ophelia's isolation and explain her madness?

7. In "Duty," Juliet's mother says, "I did what must be done. What else was I to do? 'Twas her father's word was law, not mine." She compares her duty to that of mothers in China who bind their daughters' feet. By using Juliet's mother as narrator, how does Berkman provide a new understanding of this tragedy?

8. In "No Cause," Berkman uses *King Lear* as a backdrop to illuminate Shakespeare's family life. What does *Lear* suggest about Shakespeare's hopes for fathers and daughters? Are these hopes realized with Judith? What does the deathbed scene between

Shakespeare and Judith in the last story, "Diamonds at Her Fingertips," reveal about their relationship? Is it still uncertain?

9. Lady MacBeth is generally held to be one of the fiercest and most ambitious characters in literature. In "The Scottish Wife," Berkman portrays her as fiercely *protective,* and even tender toward her husband. How does the story affect your understanding of the play and the choices Shakespeare made in his portrayal of her?

10. In "Diamonds at Her Fingertips," Will thinks, "There really were not so many stories in the world." What does he mean? What does this mean in terms of Berkman's mingling of figures drawn from Shakespeare's life and characters drawn from his plays? What does Berkman suggest about the creative process?

11. In the first story in the collection, "Gold," Shakespeare's mother prays that the Virgin will bless Will. In the last story, "Diamonds at Her Fingertips," Shakespeare's last thoughts are for Elizabeth, the Virgin Queen. How does Elizabeth help him realize his early ambitions? How do the two stories frame the collection and Shakespeare's life?

14. Shakespeare's plays have endured, at least in part, because of his deep understanding of human nature. In the stories based on Shakespeare's movements in the domestic sphere—"Gold," "Jennet," "Mary Mountjoy's Dowry," "No Cause," "Diamonds at Her Fingertips"—Will Shakespeare is as often as blind as he is insightful about the women in his life. Does this strike you as convincing? Is it possible to be a brilliant writer and a flawed human being?